I0590827

NEW EGYPT

NEW EGYPT

SOUL STONE MAGE BOOK FIVE

SARAH NOFFKE   MARTHA CARR   MICHAEL ANDERLE

DISRUPTIVE IMAGINATION

NEW EGYPT (this book) is a work of fiction.
All of the characters, organizations, and events portrayed in this novel are either products of the author's imagination or are used fictitiously. Sometimes both.

This book Copyright © 2017 Sarah Noffke, Martha Carr and Michael Anderle

Cover copyright © LMBPN Publishing

LMBPN Publishing supports the right to free expression and the value of copyright. The purpose of copyright is to encourage writers and artists to produce the creative works that enrich our culture.

The distribution of this book without permission is a theft of the author's intellectual property. If you would like permission to use material from the book (other than for review purposes), please contact info@kurtherianbooks.com. Thank you for your support of the author's rights.

LMBPN Publishing
PMB 196, 2540 South Maryland Pkwy
Las Vegas, NV 89109

First US edition, December 2017

The Oriceran (and what happens within / characters / situations / worlds) are Copyright (c) 2017-2018 by Martha Carr and LMPBN Publishing.

**NEW EGYPT Team
JIT Beta Readers**

Paul Westman
Kelly O'Donnell
James Caplan
Kimberly Boyer
Sarah Weir
Daniel Weigert
Micky Cocker
Larry Omans
John Ashmore
Thomas Ogden

If we missed anyone, please let us know!

Editor
Jen McDonnell

From Sarah

For my daughter, Lydia.
You are the real magic in my life.

From Martha

To everyone who still believes in magic and all the possibilities
that holds.
To all the readers who make this entire ride so much fun.
And to all the dreamers just like me who create wonder, big and
small, every day.

PROLOGUE

The lantern light barely lit the large lobby. That was fine, because Cordelia didn't need much light—she could see fine in the dark. She pulled her fangs from the man's neck and his head lolled back. He had been a vegetarian, which was not her favorite type of victim. Those who fed on meat had richer blood, but for now she couldn't be picky.

Turning her attention to her companion on the other side of the table, Cordelia released the dead man's body and let it slide to the floor without a thought. She pulled an embroidered handkerchief from her bosom and dabbed it on the corners of her lips to wipe away the blood. When her lips were clean she dropped the handkerchief on the dead man's body, her eyes still pinned on Hamilton.

Her partner was dressed in a traditional blue British suit, which was cut close to the body, and he also wore a clever grin. It was one of her favorite things about him.

"You always look like you've got a secret that you're deciding if you should tell or not," Cordelia remarked.

"I have many secrets, but you know most of them," Hamilton said.

"Most?" she asked, her head tilted to the side with a playful look buzzing in her brown eyes. Cordelia wore a red gothic Victorian dress, a fashion she'd fallen in love with when on Earth in the thirteenth century. Now most on that planet didn't put the same effort into their dress. Jeans? What were those? Pushing one of her black curls off her shoulder, she stared around the hotel. This morning it was bustling with guests and had a large waitstaff.

The owner was now lying dead on the floor at Cordelia's feet. It hadn't been difficult to get into his mind and make him evacuate the hotel and fire most of the staff, emptying the hotel. What had been difficult was convincing Hamilton that the Palm Hotel would be the perfect place for their coven to grow and flourish.

"You still don't like it, do you?" she asked him. His discerning green eyes scanned the walls, which were covered in old tapestries, and the small palm trees flanking the fountain and pool that ran the length of the lobby. The ceiling, some thirty feet in height, was covered in a colorful mosaic depicting the Nile River filled with fishing boats, the sun setting in the east. New Egypt wasn't exactly like its counterpart on Earth, but it was close enough that sometimes Cordelia forgot which planet she was on. She preferred Oriceran, which was why they'd decided to return to it after so many decades. Well, and it was the only place vampires could be created the right way.

Hamilton wrinkled his nose, sniffing. "It's not so much that I don't like it, but rather that the hotel smells like…"

"Humans?" Cordelia completed his sentence.

"Well, and witches, Light Elves, gnomes, and all the other rubbish who have stayed here." The lanternlight danced over the curves of Hamilton's face. He had high cheekbones like his father and the same sharp eyebrows framed his green eyes, but he had his mother's black hair and her Elvish ears. However, the silver streak that ran through the hair on the side of his head was unique to him. Every vampire's soul mark was unique. When Cordelia had been turned many centuries ago in the streets of London, a purplish birth mark in the shape of a dagger had appeared on her left shoulder blade.

Too keenly she remembered when she'd lost her soul. Most mourned for a bit when they lost their magic and became a vampire, a beast that sucks the blood of others. However, Cordelia recognized from the beginning that the change was the best thing that had ever happened to her. She was immortal now and yes, lacked magic, but was even more powerful, having unmatched strength and mind control.

Hamilton pushed away from the small table at which he was sitting, crossing one leg over the other. "The hotel will do, although I wish it had a bit more history. It could also be grander, somehow." He flung his hand in a circle, indicating the columns plated in gold and the custom furniture.

"I promise, dear, that we will trade up. First we build our coven, making it strong with only the brightest and boldest vampires. Then, when we take over the kingdom of

New Egypt, we can upgrade," Cordelia said, snapping her fingers. "Lux? Devo?" She pursed her ruby-red lips, disapproval heavy in her stare.

A tall man with two chins and small eyes appeared in the archway. "Yes, Madam? What may I do for you?"

Cordelia pointed to the man bleeding onto the Persian rug beside her, although there wasn't much blood left in him. "Devo, where have you been? The hotel owner has been dead for several minutes."

Devo bowed a few times as he started forward. "My apologies, Madam. Lux and I were trying to choose which room we would take." He called over his shoulder, "Lux!"

The other vampire's figure blurred as he sped forward, but Lux became visible when he halted just in front of Cordelia. He was much shorter than Devo, with square shoulders. His head was bald, but he had no trouble growing a thick beard. Lux knelt on one knee and offered her a hand, seeming not to notice the dead man next to him. "My lady, I hear we've disappointed you. Please accept my apologies."

Cordelia drew in a long breath and let it out as she dismissed Lux, then looked at Hamilton. "We really need to be particular about those we turn into vampires. I don't want any more duds."

Lux grimaced as he took the dead man's hands. Devo already had his feet, and they lifted the body and carried it from the lobby.

"Oh, and boys?" Cordelia called when they were almost gone.

"Yes, Madam?" Lux asked, sounding less enthusiastic than before.

"I left you each a present in the walk-in freezer. You might want to thaw them a bit, but their blood should warm up fast since I suspect their hearts are still beating. I only sent the tourists in there a little while ago for safe-keeping."

"Madam, you are too kind. Thank you," Lux said, a smile breaking across his face.

1

A scream sent Azure into a full sprint. She nearly tripped on her yellow gown as she rounded the corner and pushed through the swinging door to the kitchens. The chef, a round woman with a full head of orange curls, had her hands clapped over her mouth, and her wide eyes were staring at Manx. The pooka was in his black stallion form, his narrowed eyes beams of white light as he stared down at the pudgy woman. He huffed and put his head into a large pot on the stove.

Azure let out a sigh of relief. "It's okay, Matilda. This is Manx. He's a pooka, and completely... Well, maybe not completely harmless, but I assure you there's nothing to scream about."

The old witch was visibly shaking as she continued to stare at the stallion, who was polishing off whatever had been simmering in the pot. "I saw a raven sitting on the rack of pots." Matilda gestured overhead. "When I went to

SARAH NOFFKE

shoo the pest, it transformed into a stallion right before my eyes. What kind of magic is this?"

Azure strode forward, wrapping an arm around the chef's shoulder and leading her away from Manx, who was now making quite the mess. Split pea soup splashed from the pot as he ate his way to the bottom. "Manx is a pooka, a fairy who can shift into different forms. He's mischievous, and apparently hungry. I'll take care of him."

Matilda nodded, her eyes dazed. So many in Virgo had never left the comforts of the kingdom, and had therefore lived very sheltered lives. Since Azure began her rule she'd introduced Light Elves, Gnomes, werecats, pixies, and now a pooka into the ancient land. Her people, especially those in the House of Enchanted, were getting quite an education in diversity.

"Queen Azure, is it too much to ask to not allow your new friend Manx in my kitchen? It's a huge task to feed the House," Matilda asked. Every day her staff served hundreds of meals to those who visited the House on business. Her job made the witch very uptight, and often she could be found fretting nervously like a windup doll that had been over-cranked.

A loud clang made both witches start slightly. Manx' ferocious assault on the soup had knocked the pot off the stove and it landed on the tile floor, where he continued licking it clean.

"No, that's not too much to ask. Don't you worry—I'll take care of Manx. Why don't you take a break? Maybe stroll through the gardens and get some fresh air? It will do you good. I'll have the kitchen clean and empty in ten minutes," Azure said, ushering the older witch out into the corridor.

Matilda nodded, wringing her hands in her damp apron. "Okay, you're right. But I have to make a new batch, so I can't be gone for too long."

"I do believe if the queen mother doesn't have soup before dinner she'll survive," Azure said.

"I don't mean to overstep my bounds and I realize the queen mother is your grandmother, but she doesn't take well to not having her aperitif and soup. I've only made that mistake once," Matilda said. She wore her lavender soul stone around her neck, just as Azure once had. Absentmindedly Azure clutched for the soul stone that used to warm her chest. Of course her fingertips found nothing, because her stone was gone forever.

"Don't you worry about the queen mother. I'll take care of her if there's no soup. But knowing you, which I have my whole life, you'll make a new batch in no time." Azure pushed open the swinging door and paused, watching as Matilda scuttled away, shaking her head.

Azure straightened, pressing the fabric of her dress down, and cleared her throat as she turned to the stallion, who took up a major portion of the large kitchen. Manx flicked his tail, his head still buried in the pot. He made a great deal of noise licking up the last few drops.

Again Azure cleared her throat, crossing her arms in front of her chest, and Manx' muscles spasmed along his back. He was a beautiful creature, albeit more impish than most. When he lifted his head, his mouth was covered in green froth and his eyes were dazed.

"Manx," Azure said, her tone punishing, "I thought we

discussed not turning into a stallion inside the House of Enchanted."

The large black stallion was replaced by a small plump furry black bunny. He twitched his nose and lifted onto his back legs to show he was the cutest thing ever.

"Don't you try that on me," Azure warned, but her tough act started to crack.

"I was so very hungry, my lady. *So* hungry. And the only way I could reach the pot of soup was as a stallion. I didn't know it would frighten the chef so badly," Manx said.

"You also don't appear very concerned that you did." Azure tapped her foot impatiently.

"Who can think clearly when eating homemade split pea soup? You know that before I came here I had to catch my own game and eat it raw." Manx said this with great offense, as if it had been the most disgusting thing ever.

"It sounds like I'm enabling you by providing all your meals. Maybe I should still make you hunt? *That* would keep you honest."

The bunny's ears perked up. "Speaking of honest, you might want to move out of the way of the swinging door."

Azure did as she was told, flattening herself against the wall. A moment later a hoof knocked the door open and Blisters trotted into the kitchen as Buzz Buzz flew over his head. The unicorn looked around, his big eyes wide with excitement.

"Matilda isn't here right now, but she won't mind if we test the whipped cream for the pudding. That's my job— she calls me the 'Official Taste Tester.' Says it's important. I think it's more important than being queen, but don't tell

Azure that," Blisters said to the pixie, who had spotted Azure at once.

Buzz Buzz pointed in Azure's direction. Her hands were waving wildly, but only nonsensical rambling came from her mouth. Blisters trotted over to the oversized icebox and opened it with his horn. A large bowl occupied the middle shelf, much too high for Blisters to get to easily. Azure simply watched, exchanging looks with Manx, who sat discreetly on the ground.

"All I have to do…" Blisters put his front hooves on the shelf under the whipped cream and nudged his horn under the bowl. It slid forward a little, but mostly remained level. Blisters rammed his hoof hard into the icebox' back wall and the bowl shot forward, spilling half its contents onto the tiny unicorn's head.

Azure yanked out her wand and directed it at the bowl, making it and its spilled contents freeze in the air. She floated it back into the shelf, pushing it to the back where it would be safe, and closed the icebox door securely.

Blisters' tongue wiped across his mouth. Buzz Buzz grabbed a towel and went to work cleaning the whipped cream off his head, muttering frantically the entire time. The unicorn turned, looking lost. "Did *I* do that? Has my witch magic finally come to me?"

Blisters froze when he set eyes on Azure—everything started to compute. He backed up a few feet, cowering slightly, and Buzz Buzz flew protectively in front of him. The pixie's sparkly wings moved fast as she hovered.

"Is it too much to ask that all the hooved creatures stay out of the kitchen?" Azure asked, her voice overflowing with frustration.

"Queen Azure!" Blisters squealed. "You didn't hear me earlier when I said... Anyway, you're looking lovely. Yellow is a nice color on you. Not as nice as pink, but everyone looks great in pink. Well, not Gillian. Pink would wash him out, but please don't tell him that. I think I irritate the gnome, although I'm not sure why. Did you say, 'all hooved creatures?' Have the horses from the stable been trying to get into the peanut butter in the pantry? I told them all about it. Buzz Buzz doesn't think they can understand me, but I think my distant cousins know more than we all believe."

Azure allowed a smile onto her face. How could she not? Blisters never knew when to shut up, about like Monet. "I wasn't referring to the horses."

"Oh, well, then who?" Blisters asked, staring around. Even though he was quite short by unicorn standards, he still hadn't spotted Manx a few feet away. The bunny was inconspicuous while sitting still.

The bunny disappeared and Manx' stallion form filled the space. Blisters sprinted forward, hiding behind Azure's legs and nearly stabbing her with his horn.

"She means me," Manx said, sounding amused.

Buzz Buzz shot straight to the ceiling, a safe distance from the pooka, but when she realized what he was she dropped, her face red with anger. She launched into a series of rants, or at least that was what it sounded like.

Blisters stepped out from behind Azure. "Oh, it's just *Manx*. I thought you were a monster."

The pooka shook his head, his mane of black hair flying as he did.

"He *is* a monster. Your frame of reference is just messed up, Blisters," Azure said dully.

Manx morphed into a raven, landed on Azure's shoulder, and pecked her gently on the ear. "You know I'm no monster. Not to you, anyway."

"Stay out of the kitchen or I'll show you what kind of monster lives in the basement of the House of Enchanted," Azure said.

"Oh, threats are fun. I didn't know you had that in you," Manx teased.

"What kind of monster? Oh, no. I won't be able to sleep now. I'll have to sleep with Monet again," Blisters said, scuttling in their direction.

"There's no monster, Scabs," Manx said. "Azure is just trying to make me behave."

"His name is 'Blisters,' and if you don't behave I won't take you with me on my world tour," Azure said. "Also, there *is* a monster in the basement. If you don't believe me, just ask the queen mother. She'll tell you."

"World tour! World tour! I'm going!" Blisters jumped up and down, making a racket each time he landed on the tile floor.

Azure directed her wand at the kitchen and swept it around. The whipped cream and split pea soup disappeared, along with the dirty pan. "I'm sorry, Blisters, but I really need your help here. I was actually hoping that you'd help Gillian mind the Potions Shop."

Blisters backed up, his eyes going wide. "That's a big job, Queen Azure."

"One of the biggest," Azure agreed with a nod.

"You're going to vacation all over Oriceran and leave me to take care of Virgo?" Blisters asked. Buzz Buzz was now curled on his back, fast asleep. The pixie played hard and slept hard.

Virgo hadn't been more peaceful in five centuries. The scare of almost losing their magic had put everything into perspective for the witches and wizards. Everyone was cheerier than before, disputes were at a record low, and the good will between the Land of Terran and the new emperor, Azure's brother, had created a new economic source. Virgo was now exporting large crops of vegetables to Terran, which at first had been a strange thing for the humans to eat.

"Yes, Blisters, I'm leaving Virgo in your hands. Well, *hooves*. I can only leave if I know you'll be watching over things," Azure said.

Blisters lifted his head high, looking proud. "I won't let you down."

Azure patted the unicorn on the head and nodded. "I know I can depend on you. Why don't you go and check in at the Potions Shop? I'll meet you there."

"You got it!" Blisters bounded out of the kitchen so fast and hard that Buzz Buzz slid off his back and fell to the floor with a thud. The unicorn had blown through the swinging door before the pixie recovered from the fall, looking irritated and confused.

Azure scooped up the pixie and smiled at her. "I'm counting on you to look after Blisters. I can only leave if I know you're in charge."

Buzz Buzz beamed at Azure before launching into a long string of nonsense, then flew through the still-swinging door and disappeared.

"You're a wise and tricky queen," Manx said, still perched on Azure's shoulder.

"I'm mostly tricky, so don't fucking cross me, pooka."

Manx lowered his head in respect. "I'd never dream of it, dear Queen."

2

The atrium was full of humans and witches and wizards, and Azure found it hard to squeeze through. On the far side of the room she saw a face that more and more was a source of comfort to her. She tugged on her father's arm to get his attention once she had slid through the tightly packed bodies.

"What's going on?" Azure mouthed over the loud chatter.

"Oh, we've been meaning to tell you, but with the world tour you've had your hands full. We've invited many of the officials from Terran here. It's the first time a meeting of this sort has been held," Richard said.

Azure's mother materialized on the other side of Richard, her face bright and full of life, and threaded her arm through Richard's. She smiled all the time these days. As Queen she had always looked quietly stressed, but now she was neither Queen nor alone. Being together hadn't been easy for them in the beginning, but it absolutely felt natural now.

"Azure, it's a beautiful precedent. More and more we're opening our borders. Just imagine what you'll accomplish on your world tour," Emeri said, squeezing Richard's arm. He pulled her into him and kissed the top of her emerald-green head.

"Wow, this is amazing," Azure said in almost a yell. Everyone seemed infected with good emotions, as if they were contagious. "I'm headed to the Potions Shop, but I'll see you both before I set off tomorrow morning."

"Please do," Richard said, a proud smile on his kind face. Azure's father being in Virgo was now as normal as the raven still perched on her shoulder. This wasn't how Virgo had been before—it was better.

The leaves were turning vibrant shades of auburn and fiery orange. Azure loved this time of the year. She kept stopping to pick up pretty leaves until she realized she had a handful.

"Our queen must have nothing to do if she's picking up leaves on a leisurely stroll," Finnegan said, stopping her on the cobbled path that led to the Potions Shop. The ancient wizard didn't look as grumpy as usual, and he'd had more of a hop in his step of late. Apparently losing and then regaining his magic had put everything into perspective.

"I'm grateful that the kingdom is in a nice state, although even if it wasn't I might make time for the simpler things. I'm nothing to my people if I lose my mind due to the stress of the crown," Azure said. Just then a fairy flew out from where she'd been hiding behind Finnegan's beard.

"Oh, leaves! They're so pretty! I love the colors," Navi said, flying over to inspect the leaves in Azure's hands.

"I knew you'd appreciate them, and I think you'll love this even more." Azure stepped back and tossed the assortment of leaves into the air. They rained down on the fairy, making her giggle with delight. She twirled up through the air as the leaves fell.

Finnegan rolled his eyes at this. "I've got something for you to do, since you're not busy. Since Reynolds awoke from being a statue, he's up to something. Did you ever find out why the rogue dryads froze him?"

Azure shook her head. "The agreement was that all crimes were expunged after the rogue dryads unfroze the statues." Reynolds, Azure's old tutor, had returned to Virgo once freed from the statue garden in the Dark Forest.

"I have noticed the old crook walking with the queen mother recently. What do you know about that?" Finnegan asked.

"I know nothing about it. Who has too much time on his hands now? When did you start keeping tabs on my gran?" Azure asked.

Finnegan's mouth popped open with offense. "I'm not keeping tabs, I only wonder if keeping company with a criminal is smart. The queen mother is overseeing the court, and we wouldn't want her reputation and judgement brought into question."

Azure couldn't help but smile. "I'm sure she'll appreciate your concern. I'll pass this along to her, tell her you were looking out for her."

"No, don't," Finnegan said abruptly. Navi was now inspecting the raven on Azure's shoulder, and Manx was pretending he didn't notice the fairy. He loved to aggravate.

Azure drew back an inch and arched an eyebrow at Finnegan, who had gone slightly pink.

"If we could, Queen Azure, I think it would be best to keep this between you and me. I wouldn't want the queen mother to get the wrong idea."

Azure thought she knew what was going on here, but saying anything to this stubborn wizard was not going to work. "Well, unfortunately I won't be able to keep an eye on things since I'm leaving tomorrow. I'm sure Gran and Reynolds have only been catching up. However, on another note, I'm wondering if you would meet with Gran to advise her on what plants I should bring back from my travels."

Finnegan's expression became more neutral as he returned to business. "Yes, and I have the new greenhouse ready. I think your idea of providing a separate place for the foreign plants is smart."

"I do believe you just gave me a compliment, Finnegan. Is planet Insta in retrograde?"

Finnegan waved Azure off. "I'm not complimenting *you*, as much as the person who taught you about herbs and plants."

That sounded about right. "Yes, he is an extremely intelligent man, but as ornery as a centaur on a night of full moons."

Navi, who had been buzzing around failing to get Manx' attention, shot over and stood on Finnegan's shoulder. "She's right! You're one cantankerous man."

Finnegan brushed the fairy off his shoulder. "Does your raven need a snack? He can have this pest."

Navi fluttered in the air with her hands fisted on her hips.

"Manx is quite full, since he just ate enough soup to feed the entire House of Enchanted."

Finnegan offered his trademark skeptical look, pulling his mouth to the side. "Exaggeration is not a becoming trait, especially in a queen."

"But it's true! Manx, tell him," Azure stuttered.

With a serious expression, Manx lifted his head. "It's true that I'm a raven."

Finnegan shook his head. "As I can see." He returned his attention to Azure. "And yes, I'd be happy to advise Sari on foreign plants that would be of use to us here in Virgo."

"Good. I'll be communicating with Gran by scrying. Please meet with her soon."

An almost smile sprang to Finnegan's mouth. "If you insist."

Azure bowed slightly to the wizard before strolling past him to the Potions Shop down the walkway.

The Potions Shop was bursting with witches and wizards when Azure entered, and a bell hanging from the door chimed as she shut it. The shop had never been this packed. Were they running a sale on raccoon bile? She couldn't understand why there was hardly anywhere to stand. She squeezed past a group of witches who were discussing potion ingredients for treating varicose veins.

Above the head of the crowd she spotted Laurel, who had a large bottle of greenish liquid held over her head as she tried to get through. "Coming through. Pardon me," the werecat said. The witches around her hardly noticed her, which right then was irritating since she was trying to get by. However, for Laurel, it had been a dream come true not to be noticed. She hadn't thought a day would come when people didn't stare at her cat face. Azure had assured her that she'd be a part of Virgo in no time, and she was proud that she had been right. Now she just had to convince the rulers of Lancothy that this was true for them as well when outside of the kingdom.

"Laurel," Azure called, bobbing around behind the witches. They noticed her when they heard her voice and bowed in unison.

"Queen Azure, a pleasure to see you," the witch in the front said, standing. She had dark blue hair and a bit of beard, which Azure tried not to stare at.

"The pleasure is all mine." Azure smiled politely at the group. "Laurel, would you please help me?"

Laurel looked relieved when the witches parted, and pulled the large bottle down from overhead before scuttling forward. She placed the bottle on a shelf next to Azure. "Queen Azure, just doing some last-minute stocking before the trip."

The witches did an awful job of pretending not to eavesdrop. Azure smiled at them again, this time as a message. "Good to see you all, but if you'll excuse us?" They nodded and cleared out of the shop, making it less crowded all of a sudden.

"What's going on here?" Azure asked, gesturing at the many patrons.

"You haven't been here in a while when the shop was open, have you?" Laurel asked.

Azure shook her head. She didn't remember the last time she'd been to the Potions Shop during the day. She usually only went there at night when it was closed to help Monet stock, or just to get away from the House of Enchanted.

"It's like this from the time we open until we close. I don't know how Gillian will manage when we leave on the trip," Laurel said.

"If anyone can manage it's Gillian, but I don't understand. Why is the shop so popular now?"

A ghost of a smile made the corners of Laurel's mouth twitch. "It's better if you see it with your own eyes." The werecat grabbed Azure's forearm and pulled her through the crowd to the front, where there was a large table set up with cauldrons and bottles. A fire burned in the hearth behind it and a cauldron hung over it, sending blue smoke up the chimney. Monet, behind the table, leaned across it and pointed at an open book. A wizard with orange hair and a petulant expression stood on the other side.

"I don't care what this useless book told you. Rolypolies are of no use in an ingrown toenail potion. If you swap them out for cricket antennas it will work," Monet said, shoving the book back at the wizard.

"Next." Monet motioned the person forward, a witch who towered a foot over him. Her long flowing yellow hair was pulled back, and her purple soul stone had been fashioned into the clip that held it. She leaned down and whispered to Monet and he nodded, seeming to understand at once.

"Over there. Second shelf, third from the right. Take it every morning and you'll see results," he said to the witch. A wide grin overtook her face as she wrung Monet's hand to express her gratitude.

"Gillian, the Good Neighbor potion is ready," Monet said, motioning the next patron over.

From behind the table Gillian popped up, his head and his green eyes coming even with its surface. "How do you know?"

"I can smell it," Monet said, still discussing something with a client.

"I'm in the middle of sorting through inventory down here. It's a mess. Didn't you ever organize?" Gillian complained.

"No, I was saving that job for you." Monet looked up, his eyes finding Azure. "Queeny, get over here and make yourself useful. Get this potion off the flames."

Azure bustled behind the table and used a long hook to pull the cauldron off the fire. She set it on a cooling rack.

Gillian was again sitting on the floor, and he had a few dozen bottles around him. He picked up one, checked the contents, and scribbled on a pad beside him.

Azure knelt to bring herself level with him. "Doing inventory?"

Absentmindedly he nodded, not looking up.

"Are you going to need more assistance to cover the shop while we're gone? I assigned you Blisters and three other witches just to look after him and clean up his messes. Is that all right?" asked Azure.

Gillian pointed to three bottles, counting in a whisper. "No, I'm not hungry. Maybe later. Thanks, Laurel."

Confused, Azure's head tilted to the side. "Gillian, are you all right?"

He lifted his chin and started when he looked directly at her. "Queen Azure, I'm sorry. I didn't realize that was you." He stumbled to his feet and bowed low to her.

She encouraged him to relax, waving her hands. "You're fine, Gillian. Please don't get up, you're working."

Gillian stared down at the bottles and nodded. "Yes, and it takes my full concentration. We go through supplies faster than I can organize them."

"Why is that?" Azure asked, staring around the large shop. The shelves lining the walls burst with ingredients, and in the center were barrels filled with bottles of potions and dispensers that hung from the ceiling from which patrons could fill their own bottles with popular formulas.

"As worthless as we all thought Monet was, he's proved us wrong," Gillian whispered, leaning forward,. "He is an extraordinary potions maker."

"I heard that!" Monet said, his back to them as he helped a witch with a large boil on her cheek.

Gillian shook his head. "I've never seen anything like it. He might know more about potions than anyone I've ever heard of."

Azure smiled proudly. "I'm not surprised. That was why I appointed him Potions Master."

"I've wondered from the beginning what you saw in

him, and now I might have a clue," Gillian said, jerking his thumb at the bottle in front of him.

Azure smiled with pride. "There's a lot more to Monet than just knowing potions. If he has deceived you into thinking he was useless, you have played right into his act. I'm certain he pulls us all into the ruse just so everyone underestimates him and then is stunned when he saves the day."

Gillian pulled his brown bowler hat off his head and mopped his forehead with the handkerchief he took from his breast pocket. "Well, then he won, because I'm thoroughly shocked."

"I'm a bit worried that you'll need more assistance to manage the shop when we leave," Azure said.

Gillian dismissed her concern with a shake of his head before placing his hat back on. "It won't be like this, don't worry. Sure, people will stop in for ingredients, but most come to get advice from Monet."

"You know quite a bit about potions, though," Azure said.

"I don't know nearly as much as he does. It's like he has a special instinct for them. He can *feel* when a potion is off. My expertise is limited to what I've read in books."

"So you'll be all right?" Azure asked.

"Yes, I'll be fine, thank you." Gillian's eyes drifted to the ingredients at his feet. "My apologies, Your Majesty, but I must get back to work."

"No apologies necessary." Azure settled on the floor next to Gillian, pushing her gown to the side so it wasn't in the way. "But I'm not going anywhere until you're caught up. Tell me how I can help."

Gillian paused, his mouth popping open. "Shouldn't you be packing? You leave tomorrow morning."

"I *am* leaving tomorrow, which is why I should help you *now*." Azure extended a hand, combing her fingers through the air. "Hand me the inventory sheet. Together we can knock this out twice as fast."

3

The sun wasn't even up when something woke Azure. She peeled open one eye to find Finswick sitting on her chest, his tail on her face. She pushed to a sitting position and tossed the cat off her. "Why do you have your ass in my face?" she asked, wiping the hair clinging to her cheek away.

"Oh, you're awake! Great, we can get on the road now," Finswick said from the corner of the large bed.

Azure let out a sigh of frustration. "Very cute. Yes I'm awake, but we're not leaving until the planned time."

"You realize that you're the queen and can do whatever you like?"

Azure eyed the clock on her bedside table. "Firstly, Monet probably went to bed an hour ago. Secondly, I'm the queen, which means I can banish you if you don't keep your butt out of my face while I'm sleeping."

Finswick lifted his chin high in the air. "I, as your familiar, am linked to you. If you banish me, you'll banish a part of yourself. Hurt me and you'll feel pain."

"Is that how it works? I think you're making it up," Azure challenged.

"Only one way to find out." Finswick leapt from the bed, pawing at the door to Azure's room and opening it. "Chop chop. The sun will be up in an hour. Let's get going."

Azure rolled her eyes and pushed the large comforter off of her legs, muttering to herself, "I have a feeling I'm going to regret allowing that cat to come on this trip."

"Finswick, have you seen my hiking boots?" Azure called to the other room, where she could hear the cat clawing up the chaise lounge that sat in the corner.

The scratching stopped. "Yes. Your gran used a disappearing spell on them last night while you were sleeping," Finswick said, a laugh in his voice.

Azure pulled her head out of the giant armoire, confused. "What? Why would the batty old woman do that?"

"Because if she can't find them then she can't wear them," Finswick said in a voice meant to impersonate her gran's.

"That damn witch." Azure pulled the only pair of boots she could find from her closet and held up the knee-high footwear with a sneer. "She obviously wants me to break my neck, by the looks of it."

"Probably, but she also said you had to keep up appearances while you were on the world tour, and muddy boots and a scraggly ponytail wouldn't cut it." Finswick peered around the open door, rubbing against it. "She actually washed me and brushed me with argan oil."

Azure eyed the black and white cat. He did look sleeker. "Well, then are you planning on doing my hair? Because if not, then I'm throwing this mess into a ponytail." She indicated her messy blue hair.

"I'll do your hair if it will get you out of here quicker."

"Why are you so antsy to get out of Virgo?" Azure asked.

"I've never been outside these borders. For a hundred years I've watched over you and the House of Enchanted, and now It's my turn to have the adventure. Do you know that they have rats the size of small dogs in New Egypt?" Finswick asked, looking interested in her answer.

Azure grimaced. "That's disgusting. On second thought, we're not going to that kingdom."

"The hell we're not. I'm catching one of those rodents and mounting its head over our bed."

Azure turned and looked at her canopy bed. "Uh, yeah, I don't think so, Fin."

"Get dressed! Your breakfast is already cold."

"I haven't even ordered it yet," Azure protested.

"Yes, but I did. It was delivered an hour ago, when you should have been up."

Azure huffed, but smiled inside. She was secretly thrilled for Finswick. He *did* deserve this trip. They'd see so much of Oriceran together, but it would be different than her other adventures because there would be no dangers. They could just sit back, enjoy the scenery, and relax.

31

"I'd be ready, but I can't find my hiking pants…" Azure trailed away. "Wait, the old witch again?"

Finswick nodded. "She put a disappearing spell on anything that made you look common. Put on a dress and let's go."

"I can't travel in a dress. That nutty old bag is out of her mind," Azure said. She pulled a black skirt from the wardrobe. It wasn't exactly appropriate for hiking, but it was better than the jewel-encrusted gowns in the armoire. The plain shirt she found next must have slipped by Gran too.

Azure threw on her clothes and plaited her hair into a loose braid. She was just about to head out of her chamber when she paused in the doorway. Something on the table caught her eye. Drago's knife winked at her from the table, its shiny hilt catching the light from the fire, so she doubled back and grabbed it. The orc's hand-forged weapon had served her well before. Maybe it would come in handy again if they encountered any danger.

"What in the hell?" Azure stepped out of the House to find a burgundy carriage encrusted with bits of gold and pulled by four green dragons.

"You'd better watch your tongue when you're gallivanting about," Gran said from the bottom of the stairs. She turned back to the carriage, focusing her attention on the coachman, who wore long black robes and a large matching hat. "Are you sure they don't breathe fire?"

The wizard, who had a bluish-silver beard, smiled

around the pipe in his mouth. "Mademoiselle, you asked for kind dragons and I have delivered. These are Baltic Long-tooths. They are docile, and extremely trainable" the wizard said, his voice thick with a foreign accent.

The green dragons had lowered their horned faces and were grazing on the green grass of the lawn. They swished their tails every now and then, but not enough to create any disturbance to the carriage's hardware. Azure had never seen such well-behaved dragons.

"What exactly is going on? What is all this?" Azure asked, striding down the stairs. She clenched her long blue robes, she had pulled on, around her neck to keep the morning chill away.

"Surprise!" Gran said, turning to face her. She was enveloped in a fur-lined robe with a large collar that obscured her neck and part of her chin. "I wanted you to travel in style. Just imagine what the kingdoms will think when you show up in *this*."

"That I'm completely insane?" Azure answered.

"I was going for eccentric and wealthy."

"Gran, you might be able to hide my hiking pants and make me wear these ridiculous boots, but there's no way I will travel across Oriceran in this." Azure pointed to the carriage, which was lined with gold silk and had a gargoyle perched on each corner.

Gran looked at Azure, disapproval heavy in her eyes. "Where did you find that skirt?"

"Ha! You missed it, old woman. You'll have to wake up earlier in the morning to put one over on me."

"Please rest assured that your commoner clothing will all be burned while you're gone. Now, I've gone ahead and loaded the carriage with gowns so I expect you to change and wear appropriate dress when traveling into the other realms." Gran looked too pleased with herself. Azure should have known that the old woman's silence of late had meant that she was plotting.

"Gran, there is no way I'll sit idly in a carriage during the journey. I want to ride! And there can't possibly be room for my entire party in there," Azure said, pointing at the small vehicle. It looked like it would provide a dangerously bumpy ride.

"There's room if you and Ever squeeze in close and you make Monet sit on top," Gran said with a devilish smile.

"Speaking of Monet, apparently he's one step ahead of you." In the distance Monet rode over the rolling green hills on a beautiful palomino. Behind him Laurel rode on a mostly white horse and Ever was in the rear on a reddish apache and was ponying another behind it. Manx ran behind them in horse form, but once he spotted Azure he sped up. The black stallion overtook the rest and halted with a huff.

"What are these?" Gran asked, pointing at the horses.

"Wow, your gran is going senile," Monet said, in a loud whisper to Azure.

"You have no idea. The antique has lost her damn mind," Azure said, pointing at the carriage. "She expects me to ride in that."

"It's a perfectly adequate conveyance for a queen. I would have been honored to travel Oriceran in such a ride," Gran said.

"I think I'll take a horse, if it's all the same to you,"

Azure said, smiling politely at the coachman as he disembarked.

"Are my services not needed?" the man asked.

"No, you'll still have to deliver my granddaughter's trunks to her locations. And when she wises up and realizes I was right, she'll join you," Gran said to him.

He nodded, bowing slightly to Gran before turning to Azure. "I look forward to accompanying you on your journey, Mademoiselle. My name is Oak, and I will provide you safe travel as well as the protection of my dragons. They sense evil, and have many mysterious ways of banishing it." Oak extended his hand to Azure, which she wrung. How could she refuse such an offer? Although it did seem absurd to have this man travel across Oriceran just to transport a bunch of frilly dresses.

"Thank you. I'm really intrigued by your dragons. You called them..."

"Baltic Long-tooths," Oak said supplied. "They are wickedly wonderful creatures."

"They sound about like someone I know," Azure said, casting a sideways glance at her gran.

Ever had dismounted and stepped to Azure's side, but was not really looking at her. "So we will ride in a caravan? That seems like a smart approach."

"Orrrrrrrr?" Monet asked with one finger in the air and a mischievous look on his pale face.

"Or what?" Azure asked, intrigued to find out what he'd offer.

"Or we race in teams to the first location, New Egypt. First one there gets one thousand points. We will do it for each new place," Monet said in a rehearsed fashion.

"What are the points good for?" Azure asked, although she had a sneaky suspicion she already knew.

"Bragging rights!" Monet said victoriously, raising his finger all the way into the air.

Azure shrugged and turned to Ever and Laurel. "Fine with me. What do you think?"

"I'm not so sure…" Laurel said, staring at her horse. She didn't look comfortable riding yet, but then it took practice.

"Well, as long as you ride in the carriage in the cities, I for one love the idea. I will send word to the kingdoms—it will give them something to look forward to. Who will they spot first? Team One," Gran said, pointing to Azure and Ever, "or Team Two?" She pointed to Monet and Laurel.

"What about me?" Oak asked, thrusting his thumbs into his sides.

"You're Team Three, and *my* money is on you and the dragons," Gran said slyly.

"Wait, who said *you* get to decide teams?" Monet asked.

"Age and experience. The Light Elf with the witch, the werecat with the wizard. It's basic math," Gran said, hiding a sneaky grin.

"What about me?" Finswick asked from beside Azure, offense in his voice.

"You're with me, of course," Azure said, hoping to keep him happy. He'd been looking forward to this so much.

"Then you're with us, Manx," Monet said to the black stallion. Manx turned into a small black cat and arched his back in protest in front of Finswick.

"May the best cat win," Manx said, narrowing his eyes at the other feline.

"Well, since *poser* cats can't win, it looks like I have this in the bag," Finswick said as Azure scooped him up. She handed him to Gran to hold while she got onto her horse, then took her familiar and positioned him safely in front of her.

Azure gave her gran a look and winked before facing forward. Goodbyes had never been their thing. She'd hugged her mom and dad the night before, but there would be no such demonstration between her and Gran.

"Okay, so we're off on a great race?" Azure asked.

"Yes, off to New Egypt to win a thousand bragging points," Monet said.

Azure cast a sideways look at Ever. "Come on, partner. Let's show them how to do this." And they set off, leaving the carriage and Gran in the dust.

4

Manx, in raven form, flew over Azure's and Ever's heads. Without warning he dropped down into stallion form, making them yank hard on their reins to avoid running into him.

"Damn it, Manx! If you weren't so fucking big then I'd just run over you," Azure threatened. The pooka changed back into a raven and flapped his wings to gain height.

"I don't think you mean that, Queen," he squawked down.

Azure's horse gained speed again, but Monet and Laurel were now a good distance off now.

"We can catch up," Ever encouraged.

"Yeah, if Manx will stop messing with us." Azure angled her horse to the side, trying to get out from underneath the raven overhead.

He swooped down again, this time changing into a small black fox. Azure was just about to trample the fox who was resting on the ground, looking up at her with large eyes. She jerked the reins, nearly dumping herself off her horse.

"For fuck's sake, are you trying to kill me?" she yelled.

Manx shifted to back to a raven, a satisfied expression on his bird face. "No, but now I've proven my point. You won't run me over."

"I *didn't*, but things could change." Azure threw her hand wide. "Look how far in the lead they are now." Monet and Laurel were just spots in the distance.

"Hey, follow me. I know a short cut." Ever angled his horse into a ravine off the mountain ridge the others had taken.

"How do you know a shortcut? You're not even from Virgo." It would be a while before they hit the border.

Ever dipped his chin and flashed her a rebellious smile. "Knowing the land is in my blood. I learn it quickly."

Azure directed her horse to follow Ever. "Okay, well let's hope you're right, because I want those points."

"Don't worry. You picked the right partner for this race. Now we just have to work on sabotage." Ever pointed up at the ridge, where Monet and Laurel could be seen up ahead. Azure and the Light Elf had already made up some of the distance.

"Sabotage, eh?" Azure shot Finswick a look. "What do you think?"

"I think Monet is a snake and you should surround him with his kind," Finswick said.

"Good idea." Azure pulled her wand from her robe, directed it into the distance, and muttered an incantation.

From the sky, just in front of Monet and Laurel six snakes dropped through the air and landed at the feet of their horses, who reacted immediately by bucking and nearly throwing off their riders. It had been a mean trick, but Azure knew the two would mostly find it funny.

"Damn you, Queen Jerk-Face!" Monet's voice echoed back. Manx dove again, turning into a dog this time and racing after the snakes.

"Good one," Ever said. They sped up to maximize their time while the others were distracted.

"Will we make New Egypt by nightfall?" Azure asked.

"At this pace we will make it before lunch." Ever rode just in front of Azure, his back straight and eyes scanning the upcoming territory. It was true that few understood the land better than Ever. Azure felt safe with him. He was competent, and relied on his instincts in a way she'd never seen before. That was one reason she'd asked him to accompany them on this trip.

"How is your father?" Azure asked, pulling her horse next to his when the path widened.

Ever brought his piercing blue eyes away from the land and looked directly at Azure. "He's never been so happy. Like many in Virgo, he's been reset and realizes how much he took for granted before he was frozen into a statue."

"It appears that many have benefited from what could have been an incredible tragedy," Azure observed.

Finswick yawned and curled up, looking strangely comfortable on the neck of the horse.

"He wanted me to pass along his gratitude to you. He says now he understands why I decided to join your council and stay full time in Virgo, although he was surprised at first," Ever said.

"Oh, and why is that?" Azure asked.

"I've never stayed anywhere full-time."

"I realize that horse isn't a couch and I'm not a shrink, but you want to dive into the whys and reasons?" Azure asked.

"I believe those are the same thing," Ever argued, a clever grin on his mouth.

"Yes, finally someone gets it. I'm so tired of people saying 'the reason why.' It's repetitive."

"Wow!" Ever exclaimed with a laugh. "I didn't take you for someone who cared much about semantics."

"Let's call it a hobby of sorts."

Ever cleared his throat and his jaw tensed. "Belonging in one place always seemed like something other people did. I, on the other hand, was intrigued by new places and opportunities. Why limit myself when the wind blows me every which way?"

"Which is why things didn't work out with you and Seraphina, right? You didn't want to remain on Earth."

"Correct." Ever gazed upward to the ridge; they were ahead of Monet and Laurel now. The snake trick had worked and the ravine was easier to negotiate than the ridge, making their progress faster.

"What's changed, that you're willing to stay in one place?" Azure asked.

"As long as we're discussing semantics, willing is the wrong word. Willing makes it sound like a compromise or agreement. I truly want to be there. It feels like... I don't know, a home of sorts."

"Is that a first?" Azure asked.

"I believe it is," Ever answered.

"So back to my question—what changed? Why is Virgo

so different from the hundred other places you rejected as long-term options?"

Ever directed his horse to a pond at the side of the ravine. The water was clear here, having melted recently and flowed down the mountain. Soon, when winter took over, this would all be covered in snow. He halted his horse and dismounted.

"I think this is the ideal place to take a break and give the horses a chance to rest. We've got a clear view of our competition," he said, pointing up at the ridge. Monet and Laurel weren't moving fast and looked to be arguing, if the werecat's jerky arm movements were any indication.

"Good idea. I can send them another distraction. Thinking the winds are about to pick up for those two," Azure said, a devilish tone in her voice.

Ever nodded his approval, pulling the collar of his jacket up to protect him from the chill in the air. "Just keep the wind out of here." The only downside to being in the ravine was that there was no sun, so the temperature was significantly lower.

Azure's horse found a spot next to Ever's and they drank. The queen stretched her legs, walking back and forth several times. When she doubled back, she realized Ever had been watching her. "What?"

He shrugged. "What are you most looking forward to seeing on this tour?"

"The things I never knew I didn't know about," Azure said at once, having already thought about this question.

Ever scratched the back of his head, a confused look on his face. "Think I'm going to need an explanation, Your Majesty."

"I know about Earth, at least enough to know I don't know anything about it. And I know about the Great Pyramids, both here and on Earth. I can wonder what it would be like to explore them, to try and understand the relationship between our Egypt and the one on Earth. However, there are other things I don't even know I don't know about. I can't begin to ponder the possibilities."

"Do you mean like distant planets or cultures or species?" Ever asked.

"I do, but I also mean simple foods and musical instruments and ideas. I want to know about *all* of it. I can't wait to realize I've just learned something that I hadn't even known existed."

"So you mean there are things you know, things you know you don't know, and there're things you don't even know you don't know?" Ever asked.

"Exactly! I'm going to New Egypt first because I don't know anything about the kingdom and want to learn, and there will be many new things to learn once I get there."

"It goes on forever, this learning thing."

"I love it," Azure said, the excitement making her chest buzz with nerves.

"That was why I fell in love with traveling in the first place," Ever admitted.

"And again we get to my question. Why do you want to call Virgo home now, especially if that's true for you about traveling?"

Ever stared into the water, seeming to think about the question. Then his face changed, wrinkles creasing his forehead and his eyes narrowed in concentration. He squatted, his attention taken by something in the pond, and pointed. "What is that?"

Azure walked over, but didn't see anything until she was close. Something shiny sparkled from the bottom of the shallow pool.

Ever reached for the object, but hesitated. Azure had been bitten by enough things in foreign waters to understand his reluctance, so she raised her wand and swiped it. Something broke the surface of the water, splashing the horses as it rose straight into the air. It hovered in place, turning in a circle and giving the two a chance to look it over.

"Is that what I think it is?" Azure asked. She had only seen one in a book.

It was silver and had an intricately carved handle, a wide belly, and a long spout.

"I do believe it is. We've found a genie's lamp," Ever said.

5

A fter pulling the flask from his hip, Monet unscrewed it with the hand not holding the reins. He felt the wind from the flapping of Manx' wings just before the raven appeared beside him, keeping pace easily.

"When you indulge you slow down," Manx said, a disapproving look in his beady bird-eyes.

"When you talk, I feel like I need to drink more." Monet tipped his head back and took a long sip from the stainless steel flask. Its turquoise inlay spelled Monet's initials, MT. The incredibly well-made flask had been a gift from a patron Monet had helped cure of a stubborn case of shingles.

Manx shifted to the black stallion, his creepy beam-like eyes looking straight at the Potions Master. Normally being bullied by a stallion would have spooked another horse, but Monet had enchanted his steed to have incredible courage. He expected the horse might run across a few scary things on this journey and didn't want to dirty his robes getting bucked off.

"I thought you wanted to win?" Manx asked, whinnying.

"Of course I want to win and I plan on it, even with you and Laurel holding me back," Monet said, casting a glance at the werecat, who scoffed right on cue.

"How do you plan on doing that?" Laurel asked, skepticism heavy in her green eyes.

Monet took another drink, his mouth puckering from the warm liquor. "Well, kitty cat, the universe always conspires for me. It just so happens that I set up a meeting with a group who needs a supply of certain potions. I think I can persuade said group to help us out by creating a complication that will pull dear Azure off-course and create a serious delay for them."

Laurel slowed her horse, apprehension making her grip her reins tighter. "Meeting? Who do you have a meeting with?" She peered over one shoulder and then the other, her eyes narrowing.

"Oh, you won't see them yet. These freaks are hard to spot, and besides we won't meet them until we enter the forest down there. That's where they live, or so I'm told. No one knows for sure. Mysterious little buggers." Monet pointed to a section of forest in the valley below. Behind it the desert stretched, a vast expanse of red sand and deadly cacti that killed travelers who accidentally brushed against their needles in the dark.

"Wait...freaks? What kind of creature are we talking about?" Laurel asked, her tone now tight with worry.

Monet steered his horse onto a path that put them on a

course down the mountain. "These guys are horrible. Ugly as a horse's ass. They are brutal to outsiders too, which makes them even more intolerable."

"If that's the case, why are we meeting with them?" Laurel asked.

"For the plain and simple fact that I love money." Monet held up his flask, which was almost empty. "This herd of mutants makes a very tasty vodka that will melt your face off, and I'm almost out of it."

Visibly shaken, Laurel reluctantly followed Monet to the first set of trees and said, "You're risking our lives so you can acquire more stuff to kill your brain cells?"

"Yes, and also to help these monsters breed." Monet drained the rest of the flask. He closed one eye and peered into it, disappointment on his face.

"Breed?" Manx asked, still in stallion form. "Didn't you say these creatures are horrible? Why would you help them reproduce?"

Before Monet could answer, Laurel let out an audible sigh. "Because he likes money. Monet is going to risk our lives and probably get us roasted over a fire just because he made a deal with some savage beasts! And who knows how much time we'll lose while he makes this deal? All so he can get drunk and increase the population of a bunch of mutants!"

Monet halted his horse just inside the forest, a crooked smile on his face and cast a glance back at Laurel. "Did I mention that these lovely creatures have incredible hearing?"

The chill from the forest slipped over the group. It was much darker inside, making it hard to see what was in the shadows, but Laurel had cat vision and she recognized the figure even before it stepped away from the closest tree.

She gasped, her paw rocketing to her mouth.

The large figure gracefully trotted to a small clearing just in front of the group. The sunlight through the canopy overhead cast a weird greenish glow, which made the deep scowl on the man's face look even more sinister.

"Werecat, you dare to call me a mutant?" the centaur said. His long golden hair hung over his broad shoulders and his sharp ears wiggled with irritation. His eyes were narrowed on Laurel. Over his back was slung a bow, with the quiver of arrows strapped to a belt at his hip. His horse body was light brown, and he was almost the size of Manx in stallion form.

"Andrei, I *do* apologize for my traveling companion's remarks. Laurel is completely small-minded, and doesn't have the same humanitarian spirit as I do. I have no idea what the queen sees in the fleabag," Monet said, sliding down from his horse and pulling a large blue bottle from his saddlebag.

"What are you talking about? I'm a wereanimal!" Laurel yelled, furious.

Monet shook his head, casting a mischievous look at Laurel before facing his client.

The centaur snorted. "Ignorance and intolerance aren't confined to one species. Didn't your people lock themselves away in the Mountain of Lancothy because they didn't want to be judged for being different?" he asked, his nostrils flaring with anger.

"Well, yes, but that was only because they didn't want to be exposed to prejudice," Laurel explained.

"Funny, it sounds like *your* people are the ones who are prejudiced. That's why radical segregation occurs to you as an option," the centaur said.

"*I left Lancothy.*" Laurel's voice made the birds in the trees overhead scatter.

"I'm hoping that the werecat's behavior doesn't cause you to kill her." Monet tilted his head back and forth as if weighing his options. "That would be a bummer, and would probably slow me down."

"Monet!" Laurel shrieked.

The centaur flexed his fingers over the bow, but didn't unsling it. "For you, Monet, I will overlook what this werecat said." He looked at her directly. "It would serve you well to display the same kind of tolerance Monet has shown for our people."

About to burst, Laurel screamed, "I was repeating what *he* said about you being mutants. I'm half-cat, half-human!"

Monet shook his head and tapped the side of his head. "I think there's lead in the water in Lancothy. Not all there, as you can see."

Manx had shifted into a goat and was now at Monet's side. He studied the centaur. "Why do you need potions to breed?"

The centaur eyed the black goat and then brought his blue eyes to Monet. "I thought I told you to keep this a secret."

"Well, he's a goat, so I wouldn't really worry about it. And the werecat will probably get herself killed before we make it to New Egypt. She's never really been outside Lancothy. But honestly, I don't know how you expected me to sneak away and get this potion to you without others finding out." He held the bottle up and swung it back and forth in his fingers. "You *do* still want it, right?"

The centaur cleared his throat, standing tall and looked down at Manx. "To answer your question, pooka, our numbers have been decreasing. The centaurs are sensitive to changes in the celestial moons, so we experience vicissitudes before true unbalance occurs. This potion may help, but the true problem is that an imbalance in our magical world is about to occur."

"Sounds foreboding," Manx said, his voice matter-of-fact.

"Sounds awful. What could the imbalance be? Centaurs see the future, right? What has your tribe seen?" Laurel asked, nearly frantic.

The centaur looked at Laurel and then, pretending to not hear her, he looked directly at Monet. "That potion, it will help?"

"You'll have so many four-legged babies running around here that you'll have to childproof the forest," Monet said, handing the potion to the centaur.

Andrei tightened his jaw, but took the potion. "I've had your payment delivered to the location you specified in New Egypt."

Monet rubbed his hands together eagerly. "Man, I'm getting drunk when we get to our hotel."

"Seriously, this imbalance sounds important. Is there something we should know?" Laurel asked again.

Andrei scowled at her. "Werecat, we have seen the future, but if you knew anything of my people you'd know we don't share with others. It is our job to chart the futures, not to share them."

"But what if we could do something to help?" Laurel was really worked up now.

"Actually, I'm kind of done talking about this gloom and doom. I was wondering if you'd do me a favor." Monet pointed into the distance. "Queen Azure is traveling over that way, and we have a bit of a race going on. I was hoping you'd help me out by offering a bit of a distraction. In payment, your next potion will be on the house."

"On the house?" he asked, not catching the reference.

"Free," Manx explained, starting to look bored. He trotted away, grazing on the forest vegetation as goats are wont to do.

"Yes, I think that would be a fair deal. What would you like us to do?" the centaur asked.

"I dunno—figure something out. Have the herd charge her, or shoot a bunch of arrows," Monet said.

"You can't do that!" Laurel spat.

Monet agreed with a reluctant nod. "Oh, fine. Don't kill the queen. We just want to slow her down."

Andrei regarded Monet for a long moment. "You say that in return you'll make the next potion for free? Are you a man of your word?"

"I'm many despicable things, but yes, I can be trusted." Monet held out his hand to the half-man, half-horse, who didn't take it.

"My people don't shake hands to finalize deals," Andrei said.

"Well, what *do* you do?" Monet asked, and then shook his head. "Never mind, I don't think I want to know if it involves horse parts."

"Potions Maker, be grateful that the heavens blessed

you with incredible skill. Otherwise you'd be dead and few would show remorse," Andrei said, puffing out his bare chest.

Monet turned, pretending he hadn't heard the centaur. "I think you're swell too, but I've got to be off. Races don't win themselves. Slow the queen down and I'll make it worth your while."

Monet mounted his horse, pulling his mint-green robes out from under him so they draped gracefully around the horse.

"Centaurs do not usually play these games you wizards dabble in. It obscures our third eye when we engage in mischief. However, your payment was steep and my tribe would be glad to not have to pay that the next time," Andrei said.

Laurel looked sideways at Monet. "How much vodka did you have delivered?"

"Enough to make the next week really interesting," Monet said with a wicked grin.

"We stocked the hotel with enough vodka to drown a small army for quite some time," Andrei said, disbelieving.

"Yeah, yeah. Distraction? That's *your* job, Drei," Monet said, pressing his heels into his horse and starting forward.

"Wait!" Laurel held out her arm to stop Monet. "This prophecy… Andrei, will you please tell us something? If there is anything that we need to be aware of, a danger lurking, then the queen should know about it."

Andrei looked farther into the Dark Forest, where there was some rustling. "You know enough to be careful. What will happen will make my people suffer now, but it could devastate all Oriceran if not dealt with swiftly."

"You said that the magic will be out of balance, right? I don't *have* any magic, though. Will I be able to help?" Laurel asked, her eyes full of worry.

"You, werecat, are safe from the greatest danger, but even those without magic could be harmed. Your queen is already on a course to remedy the approaching war, but one false decision and she'll lose her footing." Andrei looked into the woods once more, almost as if he were getting a message from the trees. "I can say no more on the subject. Restoring the balance will take time, and many will suffer." He turned and trotted into the mist, his tail swishing back and forth.

"Dramatic much?" Monet asked Laurel, pursing his lips at the retreating centaur.

6

The lamp was cold and slippery in Azure's hands. She stopped herself from drying it and instead just stared at it, dumbstruck. Finally she said to Ever, "What should I do with it?"

"Rub it!" Finswick answered, looking up at her from the ground. He'd awoken and ran over as soon as the lamp had been discovered.

Azure nodded, but didn't do as he encouraged. "Genies can be incredibly helpful, but..."

"But they can also be dangerous. They are, in essence, demons," Ever said, a tentative look on his face. His eyes studied the lamp, uncertainty written in them.

"I don't think they are considered purely bad. Genies are very much like Manx. Some pookas are good and some are mean, but all are considered mischievous," Finswick offered, flicking his tail back and forth.

"True," Azure said, pondering the notion. "You think I should free this genie, don't you?" She knew the answer without her familiar's reply, but it would make her feel better to have his vote outright.

"Of course I do. Three wishes. What could go wrong with that?" Finswick asked.

"Everything," Ever said, stressed. "If history teaches us anything, it is that wishes don't always go the way the wisher thinks. For example, an orc by the name of Hoka found a lamp and wished for power. He then defeated every orc army, and nearly wiped out half the population of his brethren. The orcs have only recovered from that battle in the last one hundred years."

"That was an orc, though. They are prone to violence. Azure won't wish for such a thing," Finswick argued.

"Trinity, a Light Elf in a faraway land, used her wishes to make everyone in her kingdom supremely intelligent. They became so smug because of their great intellect that no one wanted to interact with them," Ever offered.

Azure had always been impressed by Ever's knowledge, and this was another of those occasions. "I think the important thing is to frame the wish correctly. It seems like there's always a consequence."

"Yes. If you wished for peace, there might be unintended penalties," Ever said.

"Like you achieve peace, but then everything becomes incredibly boring?" Azure asked, turning the lamp over in her hands. It had warmed and was pulsing with energy, as if encouraging her to release its contents.

"Exactly," Ever said, nodding. "And remember that every genie is different. They are trapped for a reason, and while they are our servants, they also hold many grievances over their role. Some don't believe they should be enslaved, while others remember the old lore that put them in that position. I'm not sure any genie can fully be trusted, because they will do anything to be freed."

"How can they be freed?" Azure asked. Her knowledge of genies was limited to ancient texts.

Ever scratched the back of his head, his eyes uncertain. "That I don't know. They originated in New Egypt, though."

"That's interesting timing, since that's where we're headed," Azure said.

"Not really. If the old lore is to be believed a genie's lamp finds the wisher, not the other way around," Ever said.

"How does it do that?" Finswick asked.

"It's kind of a mystery. All I know is that when the wisher has made their three wishes, the lamp disappears and reappears in a seemingly random place. However, as we've discussed, there is hidden meaning behind everything related to a genie. Consequences and extensive planning," Ever explained.

"So you think this lamp found us?" Azure asked.

"I think it found *you*," Ever said.

"But you spotted it in the water first," Azure argued.

"Yes, but you're the one holding it now. Your magic pulled it from the water."

Azure tried to press the lamp into Ever's hands, but he pulled away. "I think you should be the one to release the genie. You should have the three wishes."

Ever gave her a small smile, warmth in his eyes. "But there is nothing I wish for. For the time being I have everything I want, and the faith that I'll have everything I need as time progresses. I have no desire to mess with destiny."

"I had no idea that you believed in such things as destiny," Azure said, taking the lamp back.

"Don't worry, you'll figure me out. All in good time." Ever winked at her, hidden meaning in his blue eyes.

"That means the wishes are yours," Finswick said, interrupting.

"And if anyone is going to get three wishes, I can think of no one better than the queen of Virgo. But before you let the genie out of that lamp, be sure you're prepared. It's not just a gift, but also a burden. There's much uncertainty that surrounds genies and their masters," Ever warned.

Azure chewed the inside of her cheek. This lamp, if what Ever knew was correct—which she believed it to be—had found them. Who knew how the universe worked? But she did trust events such as this. Also, just because she had a genie didn't mean she had to use it. Wishes could go unused for as long as necessary. "It is a thoughtless man who spends only because he has money," Gran often said.

Finally Azure nodded, her eyes intently focused on the lamp in her hand. It looked like it had recently been polished, so did that mean it had recently had a different master? She was about to find out.

Picking up a corner of her robe, she rubbed it over the belly of the lamp as if polishing away invisible spots. The vessel warmed in her fingers instantly and seemed to enlarge, but that had to be a mind trick because it remained the same size in her hands. Suddenly it vibrated, making her hands shake. She whipped her gaze to Ever, but he didn't look as worried as she felt—just gave her an encouraging nod. How was it that he was younger than her, and yet so experienced?

The lamp grew so hot that she could no longer hold it. Azure dropped the lamp and stepped back just as gray smoke poured from the spout in long tendrils. They snaked into the air in loops, one after the other.

A deep laugh exploded, one that seemed to fill the land around them as if it were tangible. The smoke was now a curtain, dense and thick. Azure blinked, thinking she saw something red inside the smoke. Something sparkling. She leaned forward, conscious that the smoke was moving in her direction. Still, she wanted to see what that red sparkling object was.

The laughter was abruptly cut off by a hacking cough. A hand covered in rings reached out of the smoke and waved.

"Damn it to hell!" a deep voice said. His hand continued to wave, displacing the smoke. As it moved away they could see the figure of a man floating in midair. He was an incredibly hairy man. Still coughing, the genie waved both hands until the smoke was completely gone.

He continued to float, sitting cross-legged. On his head was a white turban, and pinned to it was the red ruby that had caught Azure's attention. It was quite large, and had been cut in the shape of a teardrop. The genie sported a bushy black mustache and goatee, and his chest was covered in curly black hair. Azure guessed that his legs, like his forearms, were covered in more hair, but he was thankfully wearing baggy white linen pants.

The genie knocked on his chest with his fist, releasing one last cough. Eyes watering and face red, he looked straight at Azure.

"For over a century, I, the illustrious and prevailing genie of Oriceran, have waited to be released. I am your servant, and you are my master. Three wishes I grant to you, and only to you. For all of time until you release me from your service, I am your devoted genie. What I own is yours. What I know belongs to you. My freedom is your hands upon my lamp," the genie said quite dramatically. He made a flourish with his arm, and bowed over his lap. When he lifted his head he brandished a wide grin, which displayed a gold tooth. "I am at your disposal. I am the great and powerful Bob."

Azure sputtered a cough of her own to cover her laughter. "Uhhhh, nice to meet you…Bob."

"Bob?" It was Finswick who asked. "What kind of name is 'Bob' for an ancient and powerful genie?"

Bob looked around, confused, to locate the speaker, and discovered Finswick looking up at him with a critical expression. The genie's eyes grew wide and he darted like smoke to hide behind Ever. In a loud whisper he said in his ear, "Oh, hell! Don't look now, stranger, but I believe that feline is speaking. I think it's possessed."

Azure stepped forward, a diplomatic look on her face. "Bob, this is Finswick. He's my cat."

The genie floated away from Ever and looked from her to Finswick, some of the worry retreating. He pointed a thick finger at Finswick. "If he's your cat and he speaks, that means…" The wheels in Bob's head spun and comprehension dawned on his face. "Holy hell, you're a witch. My master is a witch!" He was excited about this revelation, which made Azure breathe a sigh of relief.

"Yes, I *am* a witch." She offered her hand to him. "I'm Queen Azure Vladar."

Bob smacked his head in disbelief. "A witch and a queen!" He looked up at the sky, his hands clasped. "Solomon, you've been too good to me. I take back all the things I've said about you over the last few centuries." Bob hesitated for a moment. "Well, I don't take back that one thing. It was true and you know it."

Azure turned her chin up and looked at the sky, following the genie's gaze. When she faced him again he was muttering under his breath, speaking fast.

"Right, well... Bob, this is Ever." Azure held her hand out to the Light Elf, presenting him. "And you've already met Finswick."

The cat stared incredulously at the genie, a skeptical expression pinching his brow. "Bob? Are you *sure* that's your name?"

Bob still didn't look comfortable talking to a cat. He placed his hand on his hairy chest. "I'm certain that's my name."

"What does it stand for?" Finswick asked.

"It stands for nothing," he said.

"Isn't Bob usually short for Robert?" Ever asked.

Bob laughed loudly, waving a hand at the Light Elf. "Oh, that's funny. What sense does that make? Robert..." He continued to howl with merriment.

Through slit lips Finswick said, "It appears that someone's interpersonal skills suffered while he was locked away."

Bob didn't appear to hear the cat over his laughter, which was slowly waning.

"I have a feeling I'm going to enjoy hanging out with you all." Bob placed his hands in his lap and leaned forward. "Now, Queen Azure, as you are probably aware, I will grant you three wishes. Do you want to ask for anything now?"

Azure thought for a moment and then shook her head. "I don't need anything right now, but we are setting off on a world tour and New Egypt is the first destination on our list, so I'm sure a wish will arise."

Bob darted behind Ever for a second time, seeking shelter. "New Egypt! No! I can't go there. I mean, I will, can, and must do what you say, but I don't *want* to go there."

Azure shrank back a bit in confusion, peering at Ever to get his take. "Ummm...why? What's wrong with New Egypt?"

Bob peeked around Ever, blinking his long black eyelashes. "You don't know?"

"No, I guess I don't. What's in New Egypt?" Azure asked.

Moving out from behind Ever, Bob leaned forward like he was going to share a secret with her. "I have no idea."

"What? Why are you afraid of the kingdom if you don't know what's there?" Azure asked.

"Well, I'm from New Egypt. My lamp was forged there, and I have a distinctly bad feeling at the mention of the place. I don't know why, but as you always say, you must trust your feelings above reason and logic." Bob threw one finger in the air as he spoke.

Azure blinked at him in disbelief. "Wait, I don't say that. And we just met."

"I think Bob's turban is wound a little too tightly," Finswick said.

Ever gave him a commiserating nod.

"Bob, I'm sure you'll be fine in New Egypt. We all will be. And if we aren't, then I'll just use one of my wishes to get us out of trouble. It's going to be a fun adventure, and we're happy to have you with us," Azure said, extending her hand to the genie for a second time. This time he took it and brought it to his face, pressing his lips to it.

"You are a good queen, aren't you? I think I might even regret it when I kill you," Bob said, his mustache bristling against the back of her hand.

Azure yanked her hand back. "Excuse me! Did you just say you were going to kill me?"

Bob pulled his mouth to the side and looked at her with disbelief. "I don't believe I did. Would you like to wish for better hearing? I may be able to help you there."

Azure turned to gauge Ever's and Finswick's reactions.

"Remember, a hundred years in a bottle," Finswick said, striding toward the horses, who had wandered some way down the path to graze. "May I suggest that we set out once again on our adventure? We don't want Monet to beat us."

"Monet? I once worked for a painter by that name. He was a good master. Awful painter, but nothing that a couple wishes didn't fix," Bob said proudly.

An arrow whizzed through the air and stuck into the soft dirt at Azure's feet, vibrating a bit from its sudden halt. Azure stared down at it and her jaw dropped.

Three more arrows came at them from the southwest, the direction in which they were headed.

Azure retreated to the horse and picked up Finswick.

"Centaurs," he said, his voice tight. "I saw one in the trees."

"Where are they? Can we negotiate with them?" Azure asked.

"Not if they are shooting first and asking questions later," Finswick said.

A half-dozen arrows landed in the spot where Azure had been standing. It was strange that they were coming so close but not hitting them—as if they were on purpose, those near misses.

"Bob, can you get us out of here?" Azure asked.

"Yes, of course I can," the genie said hovering just beside her.

Ever had picked up the lamp and handed it Azure. "Remember to be specific with your request."

"Bob, please transport Ever, Finswick, me, and the horses to where we are staying, which is the Cairo Citadel." A moment later she added. "Present day. In one piece. On the ground floor."

The genie crossed his arms, taking too much time to measure Azure as arrows zoomed past their heads. She ducked, covering Finswick with her body. "I see, you're a crafty witch. I'll remember that during my attempt at assassination."

An arrow landed in the dirt an inch from Ever's horse's hoof, making the animal reel back on his hind legs.

"Bob, now!" Azure commanded.

The genie's face turned pink and he nodded anxiously. "Of course, master." When he clicked his tongue and pressed his head down, the group disappeared.

7

Azure nearly stumbled when they landed inside the castle. It took a moment to process the scene around them, which included half a dozen people staring at them with great interest. That was when Azure realized she was standing in the lobby of the hotel, an old citadel of the gods, and next to her were the horses and her companions. Bob had retreated into his lamp, but she'd be sure to mention this to him.

The walls sparkled with gold and depicted scenes of the pharaohs. Columns heavily decorated with hieroglyphics ran the length of the atrium, and two golden sphinxes guarded the large entrance on the far side of the room.

She waved to the onlookers. "We will just be taking our horses to the stable." Azure turned, giving Ever a tense expression. He returned it, and they grabbed the reins to encourage the horses into the open air.

"One wish gone, two left," Finswick said in a sing-song voice.

"And your ass is still alive, so you're welcome," Azure muttered to the cat in her arm as she steered around people.

"I think it was a smart use of the wish," Ever said at her side, pulling his own horse.

"Of course you do," Finswick said, narrowing his eyes at the Light Elf.

They handed the horses off to the stablekeeper who met them at the entrance. Behind him, camels were eating hay from troughs. Azure had never seen camels before, and she smiled at the newness of everything.

The citadel was located in the middle of a dusty city that smelled of strange spices and grease. The buildings were close together here, much different than the space afforded buildings in Virgo. Each building in her kingdom sat on a large patch of green lawn, but in New Egypt narrow cobbled paths snaked between the buildings, which were all tall, intricately decorated with mosaics, and painted in warm colors. A radiant glow covered everything in the city, as if it were drenched in a fiery light. Azure didn't realize she'd walked straight into the busy street that bordered the citadel until a hand on her shoulder yanked her back.

A three-wheeled bike nearly rode her down. "Watch where you're going, lady!" the driver yelled. His vehicle was towing a small cart behind it.

Azure faced Ever, who had pulled her close to him after having rescued her from being hit.

"Were you overcome by learning about what you don't know you don't know?" he asked.

Azure pushed Finswick into his arms and nodded. "You must have read my mind." She felt into her pockets with her free hand to find the cold lamp. They had arrived intact, and for that she could thank Bob.

The street was lined with carts like the one the bike had been pulling. Smoke wafted from the carts and vendors yelled to passersby, trying to sell their wares. The whole scene slightly reminded her of witches and wizards in Virgo, except that in New Egypt the people wrapped long, rich fabrics around their bodies instead of wearing Victorian dresses and robes. And this place *felt* like a city, with its congested streets and stone buildings. Azure marveled at the chaos around them.

"Your mouth is hanging open," Finswick observed, licking his paw. He didn't look too happy about being in Ever's arms.

"There's just so much to see." Azure took in the sights around her.

"Well, try not to get run over, would you?" The cat lifted his head to gaze down the busy road, his eyes wide with astonishment. "I never would have bet that was going to happen."

Azure turned to see what he was referring to, but only saw more of the same. "What are you talking about?"

Finswick clawed Ever to get out of his arms. The Light Elf dropped him at once and Finswick retreated to an alleyway, tail high and ears perked.

"Where are you going?" Azure called.

"To explore. Don't wait up. It's my turn to have an

adventure," Finswick said, disappearing through the crowd.

Azure turned to Ever. "I think I should have seen that coming."

"Me too, but now I know what he was referring to. I didn't see *that* coming." Ever pointed to where people were staring down the lane. The crowd started to murmur, and then parted. Through the steam and glow of the city, the heads of dragons were drawing closer.

"No way," Azure said, taking a step back on the sidewalk and watching as the four green dragons pulled the burgundy carriage forward. It stopped when it was just in front of her, and Oak pulled his black hat off his head and bowed to her.

"Mademoiselle, you have arrived. It appears you won the race," Oak said, confusion on his lined face.

"Just barely. How did you get here so fast? The dragons… Well, they appear slow," Azure said.

Oak held out a finger, a cunning look in his wise eyes. "Ahhh, and therein lies your problem. Appearances deceive. Maybe next time, Queen Azure, you'll allow me to transport you as the queen mother intended. I assure you that traveling by carriage is much more comfortable than horseback."

"Not to mention that I'd get the attention Gran desired." Azure indicated the crowd gathered around the carriage. Most stayed back and watched the dragons, who didn't appear to care about the gawking stares. A boy approached the dragon in the front and put out a hand.

Oak's eyes still rested easily on Azure as he said, "If you

want to retain your hand, I suggest you keep it away from the Baltic Long-tooths."

The boy popped his hand back to his chest before disappearing into the thicket of people.

Azure smiled. "Oak, I would be honored if you would transport my friends and me to dinner tonight. I'm interested in exploring the city."

Oak replaced the hat on his head and nodded. "Oh, the lady has decided that traveling by dragon suits her, maybe? Mademoiselle, I will be here to pick you up in two hours. That's enough time to allow the dragons to rest, and your friends will be here by then. I passed them on the road."

"Thank you. But... How were you able to travel so quickly?" Azure asked.

Oak tipped his hat and gathered the reins, flicking them once to bring the dragons to attention. "Oh, that is a superb question and one I will show you the answer to firsthand tonight." He flicked the reins again and the dragons lurched forward, placing their clawed feet with great precision. The beasts didn't move quickly, but rather with a practiced deliberation. Each step was telegraphed by their large hips. Behind them their spike-covered tails flicked back and forth, and their wings lay flat against their bodies.

Azure turned to Ever as the carriage drove toward the stable.

He gave her a reassuring smile, one of the many he'd offered her that day. "You're not in Kansas anymore."

"Kan-what?"

He waved her question off before pointing down the

road again. "Speaking of the heartless Tinman, look who has arrived in last place!"

"When were we speaking about a tinman?" Azure asked, thoroughly confused.

Ever's face lit up and he held up his hand in greeting. Only then did the figures of the horses and riders come into view. Monet sat tall, Laurel riding beside him. In front of them a large black dog ran, barking at the staring crowd. People looked more confused to see the werecat and a wizard with green hair than dragons pulling a carriage.

"Damn! We're a bunch of freaks, aren't we?" Azure said, elbowing Ever in the side.

He smiled warmly at her. "I'm afraid you're right. And just think—you've already added to your entourage."

"Oh, fuck. Just imagine the pestering I'll get when Monet finds out I have a genie in my pocket."

"Maybe he won't for a bit," Ever said, waving as the horses came to a halt. A stableboy had already joined them, hand extended to Monet as he dismounted from his steed.

"How on fucking Oriceran did you spitwads beat me?" Monet asked.

"I think you mean 'us,'" Laurel corrected. She had joined him on the ground, her legs a bit wobbly.

"I meant *me*. I'm the one who made the deal with the centaurs to take these assholes out." Monet stood with his hands on his hips, steaming with fury.

"You? *You're* the one who had the centaurs fire arrows at us?" Azure asked, her voice rising.

"Think we ought to go inside, guys," Ever said, steering Azure in the direction of the citadel with her fuming eyes pinned on Monet.

The crowd watched as the foreigners disappeared into the guarded citadel.

The ancient building was protected by the pharaohs themselves, as well as many spells, which was what made it so difficult for Nenet to get any closer. In the shadows of a crooked alley the girl stood, peering at the Queen of Virgo as she disappeared. Soon night would approach and the streets wouldn't be safe, but she needed to risk going after the queen then, when Azure went out again. The spying spell had done its job, and Nenet knew the queen planned to leave the citadel that evening to explore the city. That was when she'd find the queen and get what she wanted.

"You're a fucking fuck!" Azure roared, throwing off her robes. The living area of the suite was large, with many cushions on the Arabian rugs and stiff couches lining the walls. Her things had already been brought up and arranged in her room, thanks to Oak.

"Did you get shot?" Monet asked, lying back on the couch and propping his feet up.

"That's not the point. I could very well have. Or Ever. Or Finswick."

Monet peered around as if trying to find the feline, and then returned his attention to picking at his nails. "You weren't going to get shot. Don't be dramatic. There's no one more skilled with arrows than the centaurs. They think they are the arrow itself when in flight."

"Don't rely on the accuracy of the species you had attack me," Azure said, striding back and forth. She had a great deal of nervous energy pounding out of her chest now that they'd reached New Egypt. It was like there was a liveliness in the city that had infected her.

"I simply made a deal with them that they'd stall you in return for—" Monet bolted to an upright position. "I almost forgot. My centaur vodka...has anyone seen it?"

Ever, who was casually propped against the wall, inclined his head to the entryway of the suite. "There were a few boxes by the door when we came in. Might be what you're looking for."

Monet sped out of the room, a thirsty look in his eyes.

Laurel, who had been quiet, knelt and plucked something from the floor where Azure had tossed her robe. "Queen, what is this? It fell from your garment." She held up the lamp, which sparkled in the firelit room.

Azure's eyes widened and she shook her head adamantly, gaze flicking to the entryway where Monet had gone. Azure waved her hands at Laurel, but the werecat simply stared at her in confusion.

"What? You want me to set it down?" Laurel laid the lamp on a stone table, backing away from it like it was full of poison.

Azure pulled her wand from her braided, blue hair. She flicked it at the lamp, and it sped through the air to her hands. She spun around just as Monet ambled into the room, looking a bit more cheerful. His expression sharpened when he looked at Azure.

"What do you have there?" he asked, swinging a brown bottle in his hand.

"Nothing. Just female stuff. Has to do with monthly cycles and hormones, you know," Azure said, trying to find a place to hide the lamp on her body. There wasn't one.

"If you need a potion to make you less bitchy... Well, that's impossible as of now. I'm working on it though, believe me. That's first priority," Monet said, striding to Azure, who had pressed herself flat to the stone wall in front of her.

"Dear Azure, I came over to apologize and offer you a drink," Monet said, extending the bottle to her with a befuddled look on his face. "Is there a reason you're making out with that wall?"

"I'm just tired, that's all," Azure growled.

Monet peered to the side, a curious paranoia taking over his expression. "Oh, is that right?" He pulled his wand from his robe and swiftly pointed at the queen. The lamp sprang from her hands and soared to Monet, who caught it. He eyed the silver object inquisitively.

"What do we have here?" Monet asked, although Azure was sure he already knew.

"It's how I get my period every month. A girly thing. You're pretty much touching my uterus right now," Azure said.

Ever snickered on the far side of the room, entertained by the exchange.

"Oh, is this your uterus?" Monet casually swung the lamp around on one finger by the handle. "I always envisioned that there were bolts and strange mechanics in it."

Azure lunged forward and grabbed the lamp from his grasp. "Yeah, well, you wouldn't understand."

Monet squinted at the lamp, blinking. "Is there a face looking out of that lamp?"

Azure flicked her eyes to the lamp in her hand, and to her horror Bob was peering out of the spout. He popped back down, but his face then pressed into the belly of the lamp as he gazed around the room.

"Oh, fuck! Well, I guess the secret is out now." She set the lamp on the table again. "This isn't really my uterus," Azure said to Monet.

"No shit, Queen Dumbass," Monet said, hands on his hips.

"I'm going to fucking regret this for the rest of my life. Bob, come on out," Azure said, her voice full of frustration.

Gray smoke streamed from the spout and circled in the air.

Laurel backed up to the wall, looking to Ever for information. He nodded, his eyes dancing with amusement.

The smoke cleared and the genie floated in the air, just as before. "My master, you have summoned me. Do you have a wish for me to fulfill?"

Monet burst out laughing before taking a swig from the bottle. "Fuck yeah! We have a genie!"

"No," Azure cut him off. "*I* have a genie. He's not here to do your bidding."

"You're such a Debbie Downer," Monet said, striding in a circle around the genie.

"How do you think Debbie feels about her name being used like that?" Azure plucked the bottle from Monet's hand and took a drink. Centaur vodka was unlike anything she'd ever tasted. It was smooth and hot, and made her instantly drunk.

"Three wishes. How shall we use them?" Monet combed his fingers down his chin as if he hadn't heard her.

"Two wishes, actually. Master used one to escape centaurs," Bob informed Monet.

He turned sharply to Azure, fury on his face. "You used a wish for that?"

"I thought we were being pursued," Azure said. She sat on a pile of pillows, suddenly relaxed.

"For fuck's sake, you really overreacted," Monet said.

"No fucking kidding." Azure held a hand out to the genie, who looked amused. "Bob, please meet Monet, Laurel, and Manx." She glanced at the group. Manx was sitting in bunny form on the rug, and hopped over to Azure to curl up in her lap. "Group, this is Bob."

"Wait, your genie is named *Bob*?" Monet asked, shaking his head.

"Yes. Take it up with Finswick. He's confused too." Azure ran her hand over Manx' soft fur, feeling as though she might fall asleep at any moment because of the liquor.

"How about Zainab, Orr, Ringo, Usi, or Jim? Those are all better genie names," Monet offered.

"For once I agree with Monet," Laurel said. "'Bob' doesn't really suit you. I like Muhtal."

"My name will remain 'Bob.' I've carried that name for...well, I don't remember how long." Bob raised a finger decisively. "I do know that I was given that name by...well, the details are fuzzy, but it's important. I remember that much."

"Azure..." Monet said, drawing out her name.

"Yeah, I already know. I have a 'special' genie. Surprise, surprise. I think he's related to Blisters," she said, leaning back on the pillows. The heat of the room had started to put her to sleep.

"Bob, you should know that I pretty much speak for Azure, so a wish from me is a wish from her," Monet said, his voice soft. It barely registered in Azure's mind as her thoughts went to Dreamland.

"Don't listen to him, Bob," Azure muttered mostly to herself, and was swept away by drunken sleep.

8

The red ruffles on the long dress scratched Azure's skin, but she tried to get past the irritation. Gran wanted her to make a lasting impression on this tour, and she'd try her best. Why wouldn't people be impressed with her if she wore jeans and a T-shirt instead of a big gaudy ball gown? Shouldn't they be more concerned about her public policy and foreign exchange ideas than her hairstyle?

Staring at her reflection in the wide floor-to-ceiling mirror in her room, she frowned. She had never learned how to do more with her long blue hair than throw it up in a ponytail, but luckily for her she knew magic. Pointing her wand at her head, she muttered an incantation and her hair rose as if suspended by strings. The different strands wove back and forth until a wide intricate braid lay down her bare back. Azure turned, eying her magic's handiwork with a look of pride.

"Not bad," she remarked to herself.

"I'll say," a voice agreed from the top of her armoire.

Azure spun around, offended. "Manx, have you been there the whole time? While I was dressing?"

"Yes, but there wasn't much to see. Have you thought about going on an all-potato diet? That's the way to put beauty on your bones," the raven remarked.

"I have half a mind to curse you, you peeping fairy."

Manx dove toward her, flapping his wings a few times before landing on Azure's shoulder. He was a large raven, but not too big to fit comfortably. "You're missing something, methinks?"

"The fortitude to tell you to fuck off for invading my privacy yet again?" Azure asked.

"I was actually thinking a piece of jewelry. Maybe a necklace?"

Azure spun to face her image in the mirror. The red gown rippled to the ground like frosting on a cake. The bodice was tight and the dress had no straps or sleeves, leaving Azure's neck, shoulders, and collar bones exposed. She let out a mournful sigh. "Yeah, well, I have no soul stone, so unless you've bought me something I'm at a loss."

"I haven't, but I'll make it my mission to steal you some jewelry tonight. Something large and expensive, and maybe cursed," Manx said, affectionately pecking her on the ear.

"On second thought, no thanks. I don't want to be run out of New Egypt because my pooka stole jewelry on my behalf."

"Have it your own way, then. We'll have to get kicked

out of this kingdom for other reasons," Manx said, steadying himself on Azure's bare shoulder as she made her way out the chamber. She grimaced from his claws pinching into her skin. She'd tried to discourage this perching-business, but Manx couldn't be trained, it seemed.

"The scary thing is that I completely believe you."

She was unsurprised to find Ever diligently waiting for her when she exited her room. Somehow she had known he'd be there, as he usually was on occasions like this. What Azure *hadn't* expected was to find him dressed in a fitted black suit. His undershirt didn't have a collar so it was very much like a tunic, which was typical of Light Elf dress clothing. He also didn't wear a tie, but the sapphire cufflinks gave his suit a different kind of sophistication.

For a moment he didn't say a word, just stared at her like he'd forgotten what to say, but then his mouth gradually opened. "Queen Azure, of all the things I've seen on Oriceran, you might very well be the most stunning."

Now it was her turn to be speechless. She smiled shyly, then glanced at Laurel, who was shaking the lamp over the sofa behind Ever. She'd changed into a light blue toga, and was looking frustrated as she peered into the spout of the lamp.

"Laurel, are you having a problem?" Azure asked, gazing past Ever.

"No, not really, but maybe you can settle my suspicions. I've tried to get Bob out of here with no luck. Will you try?" Laurel asked.

"Bob, will you please—" Before Azure was even done

speaking gray smoke poured from the lamp, followed by his long face.

"You called, master?" he asked.

"That's what I thought," Laurel said, tossing the lamp on the couch. "He only abides your requests, which I think is for the best. Monet won't be able to use him for evil."

"Laurel, you're always looking out for me, aren't you?" Azure said perceptively to the werecat.

Feeling surer of herself now after the tense moment, Azure looked at Ever, who still hadn't moved. He offered his arm with a warm smile. "Shall we go?"

Azure nodded, taking a step forward. A loud pop made her jump backwards, though, and something appeared. Azure reached for her wand, but then noticed that Monet stood where there had only been empty space before. He had his hands proudly pinned to his hips and a wide smile on his face.

"Why yes, I'm here and ready to go," he said.

"Monet," Azure said, staring around. "Where did you come from?"

"I appeared. It's a new spell I've worked out, although the loud *crack* wasn't intentional. I'll have to work on that."

"You figured out that spell? That's incredible!" Azure exclaimed, impressed.

"Well, I have a lot of time on my hands, since I'm only running the Potions Shop and managing Chief-of-Staff duties." Monet brushed lint off his robes.

Azure looked at him like he was insane. "I seriously don't get you sometimes."

"Why, yes, I'll allow you to accompany me to the

carriage, Queeny." Monet extended his arm to her. She eyed Ever, who stood just behind him, and then smiled meekly, stepping forward and taking her best friend's offered arm. She was a little confused by Ever's new attentiveness, so she was grateful that Monet had shown up when he had.

The carriage awaited the group when they exited the citadel. Oak stood nobly beside the splendid vehicle, and pulled his pointy hat off his head and sank into a low bow when they reached him. He coughed and the dragons knelt on one knee, looking reluctant.

"Did he just..." Monet asked out of the corner of his mouth.

"I think so?"

If Gran's objective had been to get attention, the carriage achieved that. Everyone on the streets had frozen when the dragons bowed in respect. At night the cobbled roads looked different, with the firelight of the street lamps gilding them. The faces of the residents appeared warm as they stared in awe.

Azure broke the trance and stepped forward, waving to the crowd of people, who gave her a round of applause. Children rose to their tiptoes to get a look at the queen of Virgo. Many pushed through the crowd to stare at her dress, which matched the carriage. Azure didn't know how long she should wave. Should she greet them all, or was it better to save such things?

Her stomach growled angrily, and she decided that its vote trumped all.

Oak straightened and placed his hat on his head. When

he opened the carriage door, he had a strange expression on his face. "Evening, Queen Azure. I'm delighted that you've decided to allow me the honor of conveying you by carriage tonight. I promise it will be better than traveling on flea-ridden horses alongside uncouth animals."

Azure shook her head, gathering her dress in her hands. "Manx is different, but I assure you—"

"I was referring to *him*." Oak indicated Monet, who stood just behind her.

Azure laughed. "Oh, well, I see you're a quick study."

"Indeed, Mademoiselle," Oak said, his accent thick. He offered her a hand, which she accepted as she stepped into the carriage, but halfway in she froze and backed out as Oak gave a knowing smile. She stuck her head in again and looked around. It didn't simply contain two benches with a narrow aisle, as she was accustomed to with other such vehicles. Instead, it was easily the size of the main area in their suite in the citadel. Pillars rose towards the high ceiling, which dazzled with the same gold filigree that decorated the outside of the carriage. A large fire burned on the far side of the room, and floor-to-ceiling windows took up the parts of the walls not decorated with oil paintings of famous witches and wizards.

She bumped into Monet, who was trying to get in as she exited once more. "It's…"

"Bigger on the inside," Oak supplied.

"Yes, but it *is* a carriage, isn't it?" Azure asked.

"Well, it's *mostly* a carriage. It's definitely not a spaceship or a time machine," Oak said.

"And it's safe, right?"

Oak held out his hand, gesturing for her to enter once

more. "Completely. Please, Mademoiselle, please give it a chance."

Azure gulped and nodded. Although she'd been accustomed to magic her whole life, she'd rarely encountered something so extraordinary.

"I call window seat..." Monet began, then his voice drifted away as he entered the carriage. "Merlin's beard! What do we have here?" He broke into delighted laughter.

Ever joined him once he'd entered the carriage. They high-fived each other, striding around the large room—not having to duck like in other carriages. Laurel was speechless. Her eyes grew large and remained that way as she stared around the inside, which sparkled all over. The werecat jumped when Oak shut the door behind her.

"Looks as though we should have traveled by carriage to get here." Azure settled into a plush armchair that looked out on the street where they'd just been, with the citadel behind it. The view was the same as she'd see looking out a carriage window, and so much more.

"You would not have found the lamp, though," Ever reminded her, taking a seat in an armchair opposite her and staring out his own window.

"True." Remembering the lamp, Azure pulled it from her handbag. The silver belly turned transparent, and through gray smoke Bob's eyes appeared. "Bob, I know that you are nervous about New Egypt, but I don't know why. You don't have to come out, but in case you're curious, I'm going to leave you here to observe. You'll be safe." Azure set the lamp on the arm of the chair.

She felt Ever watching her with a new intensity. It was like he had been doing a character study on her lately, maybe because so much had changed since the virus had taken over Virgo and she'd sacrificed her soul stone. She kept expecting that she'd be a different person without the stone, but she wasn't sure why. It was a part of her, but it wasn't *her*. It contained her power, but that also lived within her.

Laurel's eyes hungrily soaked in the streets of New Egypt as they rode through them. The werecat was nearly perched on the edge of the window, taking in the sights. Soon, though, the carriage came to a halt.

"Are we there?" Azure asked Ever.

He shook his head. "I don't think so. This is the financial district, and I think we were going to Old Town for dinner."

"Traffic ahead," Oak's voice called through an intercom on the far wall.

"Oh, well, I guess we'll have to settle in for a bit," Azure said, wishing she'd eaten something during the day.

"Actually, we will be there before your reservation," Oak's voice informed her.

"What? How is that possible?" Azure pressed her nose to the glass window. The street was crammed with vehicles, bikes, carriages, and horses. Men and women walked between the vehicles, but there was little room on the crowded avenue.

Something rumbled under their feet and the front of the carriage lifted, putting the room at a slant. The street suddenly got farther away as the back half of the carriage followed.

"What in the hell?" Azure asked, staring out the window as New Egypt got farther away.

Ever dashed forward, pushing Azure gently away from the window, protectiveness in his every move.

Monet's face widened with shock too as he took a seat next to her. "Whoa, we're gaining elevation. Back up there, Queeny."

"I don't understand," Azure said, staring down at the twinkling lights of the kingdom below. "How are we flying?"

"I think I found your answer," Ever said, pointing out the window as the carriage changed direction slightly. The dragons, still harnessed together, had spread their leathery green wings and were flapping them rhythmically in the air. They were flying over the city, as smooth and graceful a ride as traveling on calm waters.

As the carriage slowed, dipped, and came in for a landing, Azure pressed back into her seat. This was her first time flying and, although it was exhilarating, it was also accompanied by a new fear. She'd heard of a few covens of witches in the east who flew using brooms, but she had thought that was only myth. Maybe it wasn't? She thought once again about all the things she'd learn and experience on this tour that she'd never known about.

The landing was smoother than anyone could have expected. The dragons set the carriage down on the cobbled path as if it were made of eggshells.

Monet sat close, trying to see out the window, but also had a nervous look in his eyes. Later she might tease him about being protective. The more this wizard she'd known all her life matured, the more extraordinary he became. He had a capacity for brilliance and love that few could fathom. Monet was the brother Azure had always wanted, needed.

"I'm not incredibly drunk right now, right?" Monet asked, his face pale. "We did just fly, correct?"

All Azure could manage was a small nod as Oak opened the door to let them out, a purely gratified look on his face. "Did you all enjoy the little ride?"

9

Nenet watched from in back of the carriage as the group stumbled out of the restaurant. The smell of roasted meats and fresh breads wafted from the chimneys, making the young witch hungry. She hadn't had a proper meal in a few days. When had there been time?

Behind the carriage, she was mostly out of view. All she had to do was wait until Queen Azure approached, and then she'd have her chance. She watched the group laugh. The werecat, who was a different sort of being than Nenet had ever seen before, had one arm draped around the wizard in the green robes' shoulder. And his robes matched his hair! Witches and wizards with blue and green hair?

Nenet tensed—it was now or never. She knew what she had to do. Everything came down to the Queen of Virgo. She was the key to all of this.

The Light Elf grabbed the queen's hand and pulled her to a set of shops that were still open. Everything stayed open late in New Egypt. They always had. Because of the dry desert heat, most slept in and came out late when the oppressive sun had set.

"Shouldn't we get back?" the queen asked the guy with spikey black hair and clever eyes. Most of the crowd had stared at Azure when she had exited the citadel that night in her red dress, but the women in *this* crowd poked their friends and giggled with delight when the Light Elf stepped out from behind the queen in his black suit.

"Yes, but let's browse—maybe find something to replace your soul stone," the Light Elf said, laughter in his voice. This group had drunk all the wine in the restaurant, it appeared.

Nenet stayed pressed against the carriage. Hopefully their drunkenness wouldn't complicate things for her. A creak in the alleyway next to her caught her attention, and red eyes materialized. She tensed, letting out a steadying breath. The creature moved as its kind always did, faster than her eyes could register. Nenet blinked. The alley was empty now, although she stared around. Whatever had been there was now out here in the streets.

"You're crazy. You think I'm going to replace my priceless soul stone with a strand of pearls?" Azure asked, laughing. Ever had gripped her fingers so tightly in his hand that she had no chance of slipping away.

A low chime played overhead when he opened the door to a shop, and Azure cast a glance over her shoulder just in time to see Monet leading Laurel into a nearby establishment. "Keep it classy, you two."

"You got it, boss," Monet said, giggling about something Laurel had whispered in his ear.

Azure couldn't remember having a better time. From the moment they had sat on the plush pillows at the low table of the restaurant to when she'd sipped the last of the wine in her goblet, the whole affair had been full of laughter. It was almost as if someone had laced their curried lamb and chickpea stew with something that induced happiness. Or maybe it was just that for the first time in a long while she was able to let down her guard and not worry about her kingdom's problems. Her gran was taking care of court business, and her mum had been adamant that Azure have fun on this tour.

"If the rest of the people on Oriceran see you laugh they'll fall in love with you, just as everyone does. And if they love *you*, then they will love Virgo. You have an incredibly easy as well as complex task ahead of you, my sweet queen. Make the people everywhere love you. Leave no one's heart unchanged by your radiance," her mother had said to her the night before she had set out on this tour. That was how her mum, the previous queen, often spoke—in beautiful riddles.

The door to the shop shut abruptly, making Azure jump. Maybe it was the heat in the crowded shop that put her instantly on guard. It was different than the cool breeze running through the streets outside.

She allowed herself to be pulled over to a case in the center of the shop. "Look, here are some striking stones. While they aren't insurance for your very life, I bet they have a use," Ever said, pointing at three rows of attractive necklaces underneath the glass. They were arrayed on velvet pillows, and sparkled at them.

"They *are* beautiful, but I'm not sure I'm ready," Azure said, and instantly regretted the words. They sounded too sentimental. How could she not be ready? It was just a necklace.

A woman wearing a paisley shawl bustled out of the back room. She didn't notice Azure and Ever, just muttered to a lizard who sat in the palm of her hand.

"The nights are getting longer. What happens when they erase the day? It's only a matter of time," the old lady said in a harsh whisper.

"Why don't we talk about this later," the lizard said, one of his eyes revolving to Azure and Ever. "You have customers, Myrtle."

The woman snapped her head up. The edges of her face were covered in tattoos, which appeared to start under the shawl that covered most of her head and shoulders. "Visitors! I hadn't expected that we'd be busy tonight," she said. Her gaze drifted to a crystal ball on a far counter and a strange expression crossed her withered face.

"Customers, whether predicted or not, are still welcome. Do you have gold?" the old woman asked.

"We're just browsing," Azure said, her giddy smile fading for the first time all night. There was something about the woman, as if she recognized her somehow. "Do I by any chance know you?"

"No, we've never met." The woman held her hand up to a set of baskets that hung in a row from the ceiling, the smallest at the top and larger ones hanging under it. The lizard crawled out of her hand and disappeared into the largest.

"How do you know? That was a fast answer," Azure argued.

"I have one of those faces. I always remind people of their sister, cousin, or friend," the woman said.

Azure didn't know about that. She'd never seen a face quite like the old woman's. It was long, and her nose was hook-shaped. The woman's eyes were almost black and Azure pictured her hair, which was unseen under the shawl, to be the same. And the tattoos were more than intriguing… They meant something, but what?

"You're here for a necklace?" the woman said, bustling forward. She paused suddenly, her head to the side and her gaze on Azure as if she had caught a whiff of something strange from the young witch. She turned her eyes to the lizard, who had stuck his head out one of the holes worn into the side of the basket. "Oh, now I see why we didn't know she'd be coming."

Azure looked at Ever and back at the woman. "I'm not sure what you mean. Is this is a bad time? Should we go?"

"On the contrary, this is the perfect time. You should stay, and you will take what I give you," the woman said and turned, stomping off to the back room.

"Take what she gives me?" Azure asked Ever in an undertone. "I'm not sure I like the sound of that."

"Me either," Ever agreed, moving a few inches closer to Azure.

The lizard's head disappeared from the hole and reappeared on the rim of the basket. It peered at them. "Are you like a witch's familiar?" Azure asked him.

"I'm not 'like' one, I *am* one," the lizard answered, one of his eyes darting to the back room.

The old woman reappeared carrying a small black bag, swinging it back and forth and whistling as if things had grown casual between them in the last few moments. She narrowed her eyes at the basket where the lizard perched. "I know full well who sent her here. Why do you think I retrieved this?" She held up the bag.

The lizard's head disappeared again.

Slowly, as if waiting for the lizard to reappear, the lady turned.

Azure and Ever hadn't heard the lizard speak, but the old woman apparently had.

"I'm sorry, would you please explain what's going on? No one sent me here. We just saw the shop and thought we'd come in," Azure explained.

"Of course that was how it appeared to you," the woman said. "My cousin does things in ways that make them seem like normal events to others."

"Your cousin? Who's that?" Azure asked.

The old woman shook her head and placed the bag on the counter. "There's your necklace—the one to replace the stone you destroyed." She narrowed her black eyes and seemed to look straight through Azure. "What a thing you did! Most would call it noble, although some would call it hasty. I'm not certain what I'd call it."

"You know about my soul stone?" Azure asked.

The old woman didn't answer. Instead she whirled. "I know damn well what she'd call it. You don't have to remind me," she said to the lizard.

Azure inched her hand closer to her bag that contained

her wand. Also in her bag was Bob's lamp, as well as the knife Drago had given her. Any of those might help her in an emergency, but then again she didn't know the first thing about this mystery woman.

The woman turned back, faking a smile. "Anyway, as I was saying, what you require is in there. I can't pull it out for you—only you can. Go ahead, now."

"Only *I* can? I'm not sure what that means, or what to make of all of this," Azure said, her fingers finding the edge of the velvet bag. She had to admit she was intrigued, although she wasn't sure if she should be.

"Well, it's fairly simple, Queen Azure. Just as soul stones protect their bearer, this stone will protect you in its own way. Yes, anyone can draw on the power in a soul stone, but this particular gem only protects. I'm afraid you threw away the one stone that could give you magic," the woman said.

"I didn't 'throw it away,' I used it," Azure argued.

The woman lowered her shawl, nodding, but she didn't seem to be listening to Azure. Her hair was in fact black, but strands of gray snaked through it. Most interesting were the tattoos. They licked at her chin like flames, and with the shawl down more of the artwork could be seen. Azure couldn't tell completely what it was, but it ran down the woman's neck and faded under her dress.

"What will this necklace protect the queen from?" Ever asked.

The old woman shrugged. "Maybe it won't, but my inclination is that it will. I've been waiting for the right person and time to give away this necklace. It was entrusted to me by my cousin, and she told me I'd know when it had a person to belong to. I didn't know then what it was for, but now things are clear. About like looking back in the rain and realizing you would have stayed dry if you had only remained at home."

Azure blinked at the woman. "I'm not sure that makes sense to me. Are you saying that meeting me now makes the necklace's purpose clear?"

The woman smiled, displaying a row of blackened teeth. "That's the thing about rain—it makes nothing clear, and yet we never see it here."

"This cousin of yours… That's the second time you've mentioned the person," Ever observed.

"Her. She's a her, and I do believe she orchestrated this all. Damn fool of a witch." The woman spun so fast her shawl fell off her shoulders. "Don't you talk to me about her. I have half a mind to sell you back to the shaman who gave you to me."

"Did you say 'witch?' Are you one?" Azure asked.

The woman turned, her eyes the last part to face forward. She placed her hands on the glass countertop. They, like her neck, chest, and chin were covered in tattoos. "Oh, and we might meet and not know who each are. That's the poetry of life. That as sisters we think we're different. Apart, when we've always been one, connected by the magic."

Azure nodded, and decided that even though this crazy woman was odd, she'd still check out the contents of the bag. The drawstrings were tight, but loosened under her grip. She encouraged the bag to open, and slipped her hand inside to find a cold stone and a slippery chain. Azure pulled the necklace out and immediately dropped it on the glass countertop, backing away at once.

It wasn't that the necklace was hideous or harmful in anyway. It was as ordinary as her soul stone had been—a single round stone attached to a silver chain—but that was why it had sent such a strange shock through her body. The necklace looked almost exactly as she remembered her soul stone pendant. However, the gem hanging from the chain was a red ruby instead of a blue amethyst.

"Queen Azure, are you all right?" Ever asked, taking a step forward and leaning into her.

She nodded, although she realized she was shaking, and then found her voice. "I'm fine." She looked at the old witch. "Where did you get this?"

"I'm not certain. These things just come to me, and I don't always remember how. But you feel a connection to this one, am I right?" the woman asked.

"More like déjà vu," Azure admitted.

"I'd say that will work for our purposes. Things that resemble what we used to know are usually trying to present themselves so we trust them," the woman said.

"But can't that also be deceiving?" Azure asked.

The woman clacked her fingernails on the glass of the countertop, tilting her head back and forth. "Quite possibly, but in this circumstance I'd go with your instinct."

Azure was certain that her instincts weren't unnerved by the necklace. Actually she longed to pick it up and fasten it around her neck, but maybe she was being hasty. Tentatively she reached out, her fingers pausing over the chain, then she squeezed her eyes shut and grabbed it.

Nothing happened. Well, no burning or convulsions—that much she knew.

Azure cracked open an eye and stared at the necklace, which twinkled back at her.

"Go on, put it on and see if it fits," the woman said.

"Why wouldn't it fit? It's a necklace," Azure said.

"If you don't believe me, have *him* try to put it on first." The witch pointed at Ever.

Azure shifted her eyes to Ever, who wore a curiously guarded expression. "Will you?"

He didn't hesitate to take the necklace from her. Ever arranged the chain around his throat, but stopped abruptly just before his hands would meet at the back of his neck. His eyes bulged in alarm, and he jerked his head to the side.

"Ever, what is it?" Azure asked.

"The chain," he said, twitching his arms backwards. "It won't meet in the back. It's like it's stuck."

Azure could see plainly that the chain wasn't stuck. Maybe Ever was messing with her and pretending that his hands couldn't join? But this was Ever, and he'd never do such a thing. She turned to the old witch. "Is that what you meant when you said it might not fit?"

"I think you know it is," the woman said.

Azure put her hand out palm-up, combing her fingers through the air. "May I please have the necklace?"

Ever nodded and dropped the necklace into her palm. Azure found the ends of the chain and brought them around her neck. The stone lay flat on her chest, as cold as ice but not alarming to the touch. She had thought that a barrier would prevent the chain from meeting, but it didn't. The latch met the hook like they were magnetized.

The tiny lock didn't even catch. Instead, the parts joined and the necklace effortlessly fused around her neck.

"I daresay the necklace fits," the woman said, giddy excitement in her voice. She wasn't speaking to Azure, but rather to the basket where the lizard had last been seen.

"I really couldn't get it around my neck," Ever admitted, as if he were trying to convince Azure he wasn't messing with her.

"I believe you," she said. She felt a bit breathless as she ran her fingers over the stone. Again the déjà vu moment... Why did this all feel so familiar?

"Your cousin, the one you mentioned?" Azure said to the woman.

"Yes, the one I mentioned," the woman said, finding her shawl and repositioning it over her head. "She'd say that I shouldn't charge you for the necklace and so I won't, although I don't run a charity like my relatives do."

"I don't mind paying you. I would prefer it, actually," Azure said, reaching for her bag.

The witch shook her head and bustled around the counter. She went straight to the door, pulling it open. "I must ask that you leave. It's getting late, and I need to put the charms into place. Besides, *you* might be safe in the night, but your companion isn't."

This was on a long list of things the woman had said that Azure didn't understand. "Um, how am I safe?"

The woman shook her head and then shot her black eyes at the basket. "I know, I heard them as well. I'm trying to boot these two out as politely as my manners allow." She turned and looked at Azure. "Please leave. I must lock my doors."

Azure nodded, not wanting to overstep her bounds. "Your cousin, though…" she asked, backing out of the shop. "Would you tell me who she is?"

The door slammed shut as soon as Ever and Azure stepped over the threshold, and the old witch's voice rang from the other side. "She's the one who gave you your wand."

Azure stood in the chilly night air, her hand clasped around the ruby. "Mage Lenore," she said to herself. Then she turned to Ever, who was staring at the shop they'd just been pushed out of. He rarely wore an expression of shock, which was why his face gave Azure a sudden alarm. He looked as though he'd just seen a three-headed ghost or a chimera.

"Ever, what is it?" she asked, her attention on him.

He didn't answer, only pointed, and Azure turned. The door they'd just come out of was gone. The *shop* was gone. There was only a brick wall.

10

A scream yanked Azure and Ever's attention from the vanished shop. It had come from the carriage, where the dragons weren't head-down as usual. Instead they thrashed this way and that as if they were looking for a culprit. Oak had already slid down from his bench and was searching around the carriage.

Azure plunged her hand into her bag to retrieve her wand and simultaneously launched herself in the direction of the carriage. Oak had halted and bending over something at the back of the carriage. Azure and Ever found him bent over a figure.

"What is it? Is that Laurel?" Azure asked. It had been a woman's scream.

"It is not," Oak said, shaking his head, "but I fear that whoever this is doesn't have long. She has been cursed." He took a step away to reveal the figure lying on the ground— a girl with long brownish-black hair and mocha skin. Like the witch in the shop, her skin bore tattoos which started at her fingertips and reached under the straps of her dress. However, they didn't go any farther as the witch's had, just crowded her chest and neck. And it was on her neck that Azure saw them: the punctures. They were bright red and blood snaked down her throat to puddle at her collarbone. The girl's dark-green eyes fluttered opened.

"Queen Azure…" she whispered, extending her hand, which was covered in gold jewelry, toward Azure. Behind them the flapping of wings drew their attention. Azure spun, expecting to find Manx, but there was only the black of the alleyway.

Azure turned back around. "Put her in the carriage. We must get out of here now."

"But Queen Azure, she's been cursed. You know what these marks mean, do you not?" Oak questioned.

"I've never seen them in real life, but yes, I absolutely do. As I said before, load her into the carriage." Azure turned to Ever. "Would you please find Monet, Laurel, and Manx? Tell them we're leaving very soon."

He nodded. "I'll be back in a moment. Don't worry, I'll bring them with me." Ever left and Azure stared at the girl on the brick road. Oak had still not moved her.

"Oak!" Azure snapped as she glanced at him. "I asked you to take her to the carriage. Please do as I said." Behind her Azure heard the flapping of wings again, and this time she knew for a fact that it wasn't Manx.

"Queen, you know I will do anything that you say, but this witch has been cursed. We don't have long," Oak warned.

"Yes, she's been bitten by a vampire, which is why we must try and save her before she becomes a Forsaken.

Move her to the carriage *now*." Azure spun, putting her back to the girl and Oak, her wand at the ready.

"You'll be safe from whatever is out there inside the carriage," Oak said, standing on the ground and looking up at Azure, "but I can't assure that you're safe from *her* inside the carriage." He pointed to the woman, who was lying across the sofa in the middle of the room.

"I'll be fine," Azure reassured him.

"I'll get the dragons ready to go for when your friends return," Oak said, tipping his hat to the queen before closing the door.

The girl muttered in her sleep. Was she really sleeping? Was she actually slipping away? Her hair was damp with sweat, and she tossed her head back and forth like she was wrestling a demon in her dreams.

Azure had never seen someone who had been bitten by a vampire, since the epidemic had been eradicated years before she was born. She'd heard rumors of rogue vampires who had escaped imprisonment, but the founder vampires had been wiped out—at least according to the records. *They* were the dangerous ones. The ones who were truly to be feared. This girl would become a follower, which was what a bite from a founder vampire did. It turned magical beings into followers. Azure suspected the girl had been bitten by a founder, because she'd heard the beating of wings. Bat wings, she suspected. That was one of the many gifts the founders possessed: the ability to transform into bats.

The door to the carriage flew open, making Azure jump. "I heard you lost your damn mind, but now I see it with my own eyes." Monet raced over, putting himself between Azure and the girl, his wand in the hand pointed at the soon-to-be vampire.

"I couldn't just leave her there," Azure argued. "She'd just been bitten."

"I agree. You shouldn't have just left her there. You should have killed her." Monet's eyes were trained on the girl, but his words had been intended for Azure.

"How can you say that? I know you're not cruel."

"No, I'm not. I'm kind, despite what most believe, and a life spent feeding on mammals isn't an existence I'd wish for the vilest of wizards. That's the life this girl now has stretching in front of her," Monet said. He was madder than Azure had ever seen him. His wand-hand was steady, but his voice was shaking.

"Not to mention that she carries the virus," Laurel interjected. "Her venom will kill whoever she feeds on in time even if she doesn't."

"That's what the books dictate, but I've never seen a case of vampirism. Laurel, have you?" Azure asked.

"Well, no. I only also know this from reading," the werecat said as Ever shut the door behind him. His eyes rested on the figure lying on the couch with a strangely ungallant expression.

"There hasn't been a case in over a hundred and fifty years," Ever informed them.

"Exactly, which means that things could have changed. There might be options and solutions we didn't have before. Maybe this time…" Azure's voice trailed off as she thought hard.

"Vampires don't have to be killed or imprisoned," he finished her sentence.

"Yes. Maybe things can be different. Maybe we can handle vampires differently than our ancestors did," Azure said.

Monet dared to take a few steps closer to the stranger on the couch. He knelt and picked up her arm, feeling for a pulse.

"Queen Azure, should you really risk helping a vampire? You have a kingdom. I salute your nobility, but shouldn't someone else champion a cure?" Laurel asked as the carriage took off, nearly knocking them all to the floor from the sudden lurch.

"If not me, who has vast resources and incredible talent at my disposal, then who? What is the point in leading people only to abandon those who truly need help?" Azure asked, sounding genuinely offended.

"I was merely saying that your power could be compromised. The crown," Laurel said, standing her ground.

And the werecat was right. If Azure's gran learned she was considering such a thing, she'd advise her against it. This put everyone in danger. A queen should be as far from the follower vampire virus as possible. Being bitten by this stranger would kill Azure and everyone in the carriage. "What is more concerning than the loss of power is that this is the first known case of vampirism in over a century. Where we have a follower vampire, we know that there is a founder."

"Do you believe they wanted to turn her, this founder?" Ever asked, his voice careful.

"I do, and I intend to learn more, but we'll have to wait until this girl awakes," Azure said, her eyes resting thoughtfully on the witch, who stirred more violently now in her comatose state.

"Well, that won't be long." Monet dropped the girl's wrist. "Her pulse has stopped. She's officially dead now."

A deep frown wrinkled every part of Azure's face with sadness. She hadn't known the girl, but that didn't mean she was exempt from mourning the death of a fellow witch, or a creature of any sort.

"She'll have lost all her magic when she rises," Ever said, his voice clinical.

"But she'll be immortal. A nice perk of being a follower," Monet said.

"Not worth losing one's magic, I'd say." Ever crossed his arms, and his expression said this was a personal insult.

"Well, as someone without magic, I think that it's a fair trade. Followers are also granted enhanced speed and agility," Laurel said, musing on this idea in a scientific tone. Yes, turning a wereanimal into a follower vampire would have few disadvantages, but the historical cases proved that most went rabid, unable to control being fused with magic and bat DNA. Vampirism was a complex virus that not all host bodies handled well. The results among species varied.

"Is there anything you can do to save her at this point?" Azure asked Monet.

"I'm not the one who has a personal genie in my pocket." Monet pointed to the bag Azure held.

Excitement overwhelmed Azure's chest. Genie! It was fucking perfect. She stuck her hand in to the bag and withdrew the lamp. "Bob, I have a wish for you to grant."

Just as before, gray smoke rose a few feet in the air and his round face appeared. Bob sputtered out a cough, clapped himself on the back, and waved his hand to clear the smoke. "I really have to find a different way to make an appearance. This smoke is awful for my lungs, not to mention that it makes me smell like a campfire."

"You have lungs? I thought you were a—"

Azure cut Monet off with a single look. "We have an issue. I need your help." She pointed to the passed-out girl. "She's been bitten by a founder vampire and is about to change. I wish for you to save her, make her a human once more, and prevent her from ever becoming a vampire."

Bob crossed his thick arms in front of his chest and shook his head. "No can do. Article Six of Section Seven of the Genie Bylaws states that we can't bring anyone back from the dead."

"But she *just* died," Azure complained.

"'Just' doesn't matter. The fact remains that the girl is dead, and I can't bring her back to life. My hands are tied."

"Fine, then prevent her from becoming a vampire. You can do that, right?" Azure asked.

Again the genie shook his head. "Vampires are protected in our bylaws under Section Twelve."

"You've got to be kidding me," Monet scoffed. "Vampires are a protected class in your bylaws?"

"All species are protected. I can't change you into a Light Elf or turn a canary into a wizard," Bob explained.

"Why would someone want to turn a canary... Never

mind," Monet said, waving him off.

"You can't save her or keep her a witch. What *can* you do?" Azure asked.

"I can serve her a thick juicy steak and a bottle of Chianti when she wakes up," Bob said, proud of himself. "Just make that wish and it will be done."

"No deal." Azure stared intently at the girl, her head clouded by this new situation.

"Would you like a foot rub? Ice cream? A coffin with your initials on it?" Bob held up a gold ringed-finger for each of the things he listed.

"A coffin? For me?" Azure asked, confused.

"Oh," Bob squeaked, "of course not. I meant for the witch who is about to be a vampire. They hate the sun. I could get her a hat. Just make the wish."

Monet strolled over and whispered loudly. "I heard him say, 'coffin with *your* initials on it.'"

"Yes, my genie is out to get me. That's just my luck," Azure muttered as the carriage slowed.

"Master, I only want what's best for you. You're my master, who I'm bound to no matter what and must respond to without fail, so why would I want anything but the best for you?" Bob floated up a few inches and then down again with an amused look on his face.

Azure was too far off in thought to be concerned with the sadistic genie. "Monet and Ever, would you please carry the girl up to the room?"

"First off, you want to take a newbie follower vampire up to our room? I don't have to tell you what a bad idea that is," Monet stated.

"Fine. Ever, will you do it? I'll help you." Azure looked

at the Light Elf, who wore a stony expression. He didn't budge when the carriage came to a halt.

"I actually agree with Monet on this. I know you want to help, but there's no cure for vampirism. We'll all be in danger if you take her with us," Ever said, looking like he was punishing himself for his words.

"See? Even though he's obsessed with you, Ever still opposes this horrible idea of yours," Monet said.

"Shut up, Monet," Azure spat.

Ever gave her a pleading expression. "I appreciate that you want to help this girl, but one bite from her and we will have the virus, which we can't recover from. It's deadly. You know that only founders can turn people into vampires, right? Followers just infect."

"But not if she's restrained and fed," Azure stated, having mostly thought it out.

"And second," Monet said loudly, "how are you going to get a dead girl through the lobby of the citadel to the room?"

Azure pointed her wand at the girl and whirled it. "Anyone draped on you at this hour, Monet, is obviously drunk." The witch levitated toward Monet horizontally before going vertical. Her arm hung over his shoulder, and her head lolled forward. She just looked like she'd had a bit too much centaur vodka, and her long black hair covered the bitemarks on her neck.

Monet narrowed his eyes at Azure, but secured the girl before she slipped off. Ever picked up her other arm and pulled it around his shoulder.

"Okay, I guess we're really doing this," Azure said, turning to the door just as Oak opened it.

11

Laurel mopped a rag across the girl's forehead, humming a strange tune. From her kneeling position next to the sofa Azure looked up at the werecat, who appeared to be in a trance. She was a natural caregiver, who had already tended many of the animals and residents in Virgo.

"What is that song you're humming?" Azure asked. It was a spellbinding melody.

"It's a lullaby from Lancothy. We sing it to our young and our sick," Laurel said, squeezing the rag out into a bowl. The girl had stopped sweating about the time her heart stopped, but Laurel had been adamant about mopping her forehead with the wet rag.

Azure's eyelids started to slip closed as Laurel continued humming. "It's enchanting. Makes me sleepy." She swayed on her heels a bit.

"We don't have magic as wereanimals, but we have our own brand of power—a long tradition of songs, herbs, and other practices that have properties like magic. This lullaby was created to soothe and put people at ease." Laurel resumed her humming as soon as she was done speaking.

Azure placed her hand on the werecat's arm and shook her head. "Although I appreciate your attempts to soothe our guest, please stop singing unless you want me to fall over."

Laurel didn't answer, just went quiet. She sprinkled a drop of the oil that was next to her on the rag and mopped it across the girl's head. The stranger was now perfectly still, her skin pale.

"What's that oil?" Azure asked.

"It's bay leaves, an herb known to combat anxiety. It fills the places we think are missing so we don't feel like we have lost something, which is where many stresses come from," Laurel explained, rocking back and forth as if she were still humming in her head.

"Do you often treat the person's psychological state rather than the ailment?" Azure observed.

"We are really only thoughts. Our physical manifestation comes from the thoughts we have, which are often triggered by our emotions. In were-animal medicine we treat the emotions first."

"If you hens would stop clucking about voodoo for a moment, I have a logical concern," Monet interrupted from the far side of the room, rummaging through a bag he'd brought. "How do you know that the restraining charm you put on this broad will work when she awakes? What if it won't hold her down because it doesn't work on vampires?"

"There's only one way to find out," Azure said as she

stood. "Laurel, you should step back, though, in case Monet is right. A little distance would be good."

Laurel didn't argue, although she didn't look the least bit worried. She gathered her materials and went toward her room, where she kept her essential oils.

A whistle caught Azure's attention and she looked at Monet, who tossed a clear bottle filled with crimson liquid at her. She held it up to the fire and read the label: Rabbit's blood.

"What do you want me to do with this?" Azure asked, but the answer dawned on her at that moment. "Oh, you think?"

"I think she'll be hungry, and although she might *prefer* human blood, from everything I've read vampires just need blood." Monet continued rummaging through his bag, pulling out other bottles of red liquid.

"Well, although you're against this idea, thanks for being helpful," Azure said, her hands shaking slightly as she stared at the frozen figure of the girl who would soon awaken as a monster. She'd never been around a vampire, but the lore was consistent. They were savage beasts, owned by the night and their hunger for blood. But they were still people—or at least they had been.

"You won't thank me if you come down with a serious ailment that requires blood for the cure, because I'll probably be all out." Monet withdrew another bottle from his bag and stood back, looking at the six bottles. That was all the blood he had packed, all from different animals.

A loud and chilling scream ripped from the girl's mouth and she bolted upright, her olive-green eyes springing open. Sharp fangs dropped from either side of her upper jaw, and she tried to lunge forward. However, her arms remained pinned to her sides and her legs were glued together in front of her. The girl screamed again, then snarled. Azure's binding charm was keeping her in place.

Laurel had returned, and fear blanketed her expression. She and Azure both shot back several feet to put some space between them and the vampire. Now Azure dared to step forward, leaning down.

"I wouldn't…" Ever started, but his voice trailed off after the warning look Azure threw at him. He held up his hands in surrender.

Monet nodded at the Light Elf. "There's no swaying her once she's made up her mind."

"It's kind of what I like about her," Ever replied.

The girl screamed again, and then a white mark sliced through the middle of one of her green eyes,. It instantly made her appear different. Otherworldly. Immortal.

"That's a soul mark," Laurel said, pointing to the girl's eye. She was well read, and it was proving useful in this situation.

"The mark shows that her soul has left her for good," Azure confirmed, pity in her voice.

Laurel nodded, weight in the movement.

The vampire panted like she'd just run a long distance. Her crazed stare shot in ten different directions, as if she were being tortured by distant voices.

Azure held the bottle of blood in front of the vampire, which got her attention at once. She sniffed the air and trained her eyes on it. "You're hungry, aren't you? That's how this transition works, isn't it? You're a vampire now. You know that, right?"

The vampire didn't seem to hear her, just dropped her eyes when Azure placed the bottle on the ground.

Azure raised her wand and swiped it and the bottle rose and floated over to the vampire. Her eyes enlarged with hungry delight as it neared her face. The cork pulled out of the top when it was next to the girl's mouth, and it tilted forward. The girl drank hungrily, and a few seconds later the blood was gone. She tore her face away from the floating bottle and the ravenous heat started to drain from her eyes.

Before them, the girl transformed. She had been beautiful before, but now she became something more. Her long straight black hair shrank into gorgeous shiny curls. Her cocoa skin glowed slightly, like it shimmered with bits of diamond. The tattoos on her skin disappeared, and her body slimmed. The features on the vampire's face changed ever so slightly until they complimented each other perfectly. She blinked at the three in front of her and her eyes glowed slightly, the white streak in her right eye extra-bright.

"Queen Azure, I came to warn you. I was waiting for you so that I could ask for your help, but now it's too late. I've failed you, and I've failed my coven," the girl said. She twisted, but was not able to move because of the invisible bindings. A new solemnity came to the girl's face, and her words were slow and full of grief.

"Warn me? What are you talking about?" Azure asked. "Is this about the founder vampire?"

The girl shook her head, but then nodded as if she'd changed her mind. Azure could tell that pure sorrow shrouded her mind. This was not someone who had wanted to be a vampire. Who would?

"Let's back up," Azure said, whirling her wand. The girl's hands fell away from her sides and her legs relaxed.

"What are you doing? You took the bonds off her?" Monet bolted forward, placing himself in front of Azure.

Laurel set a paw on his arm. "It's all right. She's not dangerous as long as she's not hungry—that much is obvious. Azure was right to free her."

"We can learn just as much with her restrained as not," Monet said bitterly.

"But we don't gain trust that way." Azure turned back to the vampire. "You know I'm the queen of Virgo. Who are you?"

The girl swallowed, her eyes skirting around the room as if watching a fly buzzing through the space. "I'm Nenet. I'm with a coven as old as Old Egypt, and I was sent to tell you to be on guard."

"Because there's a founder vampire in the city. The one who got you, correct?" Azure asked.

Nenet shook her head. "There's not just one founder vampire, there are two. They're taking over the kingdom, and have turned many into followers. And now one of the founders has turned me." The young witch buried her head in her hands and began to sob softly. Azure stepped forward and took a seat next to the girl, folding her in her arms.

"I'm so sorry. I can only imagine how hard this is to deal with. We can help you. Where is your coven? We'll take you to them," Azure said thoughtfully.

Still crying, Nenet shook her head. "They won't want

me. I'm Forsaken. I have no magic, and I'll forever be controlled by the hunger."

Azure looked up at Monet and inclined her head to the table where the bottles filled with blood were sitting. He took the hint and flicked his wand, making the nearest bottle fly to him. Cautiously he handed it to Azure.

"Nenet, you're not a danger as long as you're not hungry. I know that much of follower vampires. Here." She took the girl's hand from her crying face and unfurled her fingers, laying the bottle of blood in her palm. "Take this. We have more, and we will get you as much as you need for as long as you need. When you get hungry, drink this blood and you won't be a danger to anyone."

Nenet shook her head adamantly, but then stopped herself, a pained smile on her tortured face. "Thank you, but that won't be enough. As a follower vampire I'll be summoned to my master soon. The founder who turned me has only to request my presence and I'll have no choice but to find them."

Azure's mouth popped open. She looked up at Monet like his face might make sense of this new information. "Is that how it works?"

"Yes. The founders own the followers," Nenet answered, "and the followers feed and spread the deadly virus. This is a growing problem in New Egypt. We lost so many with magic to the virus, and we've lost even more to vampirism. And now I…" Nenet sobbed again.

"The imbalance," Laurel said in a hushed voice, gaining everyone's attention.

"What did you just say?" Azure asked.

"The centaurs spoke of an imbalance that would affect

everyone. Andrei said it couldn't completely affect me because I don't have magic. I can't become a founder, but I *could* be turned into a follower, although I wouldn't survive it. And the virus could still kill me. No one is immune to that," Laurel said.

Monet slammed his open palm to his forehead. "Oh fuck, and he said that bit about Azure."

Azure spun to look at him. "What bit?"

Laurel drew in a loud breath. "He said that you were already on a course to remedy the approaching war, but one false decision and you'd lose your footing."

Azure turned to Nenet, who was still mourning the loss of her humanity. "You said your coven sent you to find me and I could help. I need you to take me to your coven now."

12

The streets were buzzing with people as the group snuck through the alleyways.

"All these people should be inside away from vampires," Nenet said, a piece of fabric wrapped around her head and draped over her shoulders as she led the way through New Egypt.

"Are the vampires common knowledge?" Azure asked.

"Yes, but no one truly believes it. Those who have been personally affected, yes, but even they have been hard to convince. It's just not a problem we're equipped to handle. You remember how the last epidemic was dealt with?" Nenet asked, halting the group with a hand movement while checking the busy street ahead.

Azure nodded. It had been brutal—a war that had hardly been documented. Maybe only the gnomes in the Light Elf library knew the true details. Azure made a mental note to scry Gillian and find out what he remembered about the history.

The buildings thinned as they came to the outskirts of the city, where the desert overwhelmed the land. Azure sucked in a breath when she looked over a mostly flat plain at three giant pyramids. Buildings were sprinkled behind the structures, but the largest of the pyramids monopolized the view. The light of the half-moons made it very noticeable. The vampire grabbed Azure's wrist and pulled her in the direction of the pyramids, nearly dragging her in her intensity.

Azure pulled back, dropping her weight into her heels. She pointed at the largest pyramid, which created a strange, foreboding feeling in her chest. "Is that where your coven is located? You said they were as old as New Egypt."

"The Great Pyramid of Giza is older than our history, it is true. The first was built on Earth. However, no, that's not our headquarters. My coven resides there." Nenet indicated the giant Sphinx, whose outline was also visible.

Nenet picked up the pace, hurrying across the desert. She moved faster than the rest of the group due to her vampirism, but she kept her pace manageable so everyone could stay with her. Manx had no problem as a raven.

Twice Nenet checked the horizon where the sun would be rising in a few hours over her shoulder, and each time there was a strange intensity in her gaze. Vampires couldn't tolerate the sun but it wasn't clear why, Azure remembered as she was led across the dusty desert. The sand wasn't thick, and she was glad for that.

"It's because of Ra," Nenet whispered.

Azure was unsure if she'd heard her right. "What?"

"You were wondering why vampires can't tolerate the

sun. It's because the Sun God Ra cursed us," Nenet explained in a low voice.

"You heard my thoughts?" Azure asked, slightly repulsed.

"I guess I did, but it felt like you were speaking out loud," Nenet said, taking her hand off Azure's wrist. She was introspectively silent for a moment. "It must have been because I was touching you, since I don't hear your thoughts now. And I sense that once my vampirism sets in I won't be *able* to touch you. Even now I feel repelled. It's a strange sensation that's setting in more quickly with each passing minute."

Azure brushed her hand over her arm as if wiping away the connection. She felt the others tense behind her. Being with a vampire wasn't safe, and even *she* had to admit it. Apparently they had been given telepathy linked to touch along with their enhanced speed, or at least followers did. The founders were no doubt even more powerful.

"You said Ra cursed the vampires. Can you explain more about the Egyptian connection to vampirism?" Laurel asked.

"I can't, but my coven can. It's where I learned everything that I know." Nenet sped up, closing the distance to the Sphinx. "Usually we're required to be invisible when nearing and entering our headquarters, but I no longer have magic."

"And we don't have invisibility charms," Ever stated.

"Speak for yourself," Monet said. He pulled out his wand and waved it at the group. "*Invisibilia.*"

Ever, Azure, and Monet turned invisible.

"What?" Azure asked. "When were you going to share these spells with me?"

"Surprise!" the bodiless voice of Monet said.

"Why aren't Laurel or Nenet invisible?" Ever asked.

"Probably because they don't have magic," Monet said.

"It doesn't matter. The leader of my coven will be so angry with me that being visible when entering the headquarters will be the last of his concerns." Nenet sounded dejected.

As they neared the Sphinx, the gold and blue of the pharaoh's headdress was the first thing to come into view. The head had been carved with incredible details, including a magnificent braided beard and discerning eyes. The body was massive, with long front paws, a giant body, and tall hind legs.

Azure thought they'd run for an area between the front paws, but Nenet stopped several yards from the Sphinx and disappeared into the ground. A moment later Azure realized that there was an underground passage for those who knew how to look. Carefully the group descended the stairs, which were almost completely cast in blackness.

The steps were narrow, and several times Azure almost slipped. She ran her hands down the stone wall for stability. It wasn't until they had come to an open room that the torches on the walls gave them any sight. Nenet turned at once and stared at Azure.

"I leave you here. Go to the stone door ahead and you will be granted access. Your witch blood is all you need," she said.

"What about you?" Azure asked.

"I can go no farther. The Sphinx is guarded from my kind," Nenet said.

Azure gulped at the phrase, "My kind." In one night, the witch before her had lost everything. She was never going to have magic again. She was separate from her people. Becoming a vampire had changed everything for Nenet.

"Ask to see Chibale. He will explain everything that I can't." Nenet kept looking at the stairs that led to the desert, where the sun would soon be rising. Did she have enough time to get to safety? And where would that be found?

"Where will you go?" Azure asked.

Nenet blinked, shame in her expression. "I've been summoned. I cannot resist it much longer."

"Oh." Azure hiccupped on the word.

"Your founder," Laurel guessed.

The weight of Manx' raven form landing on Azure's shoulder nearly made her jump. "Maybe you can stay. Maybe there's something we can do for you," Azure said.

"I'm hoping you *can* help me. We're all hoping you can, but I can't stay to find out. Chibale will have to fill you in on the history. Queen Azure, whatever happens, stay away from the bats," Nenet said with conviction. She looked deeply into Azure's eyes before scanning the group, then she was a blur, speeding from the room as only a vampire could.

In cat form Manx led the way to the stone arch, which was flanked by torches set in golden brackets. A door stood before the group. Wait, *was* it a door? The closer they got, the more transparent it appeared. At an angle, a hallway could be seen on the other side. If you turned your head the other way, the door was solid stone.

Azure paused only a few inches from the door/not door. "What do you make of this?"

"Maybe it's a test, and we have to complete the right tasks to get through," Manx offered.

"Maybe it's a door and we have to knock," Laurel said.

"Maybe it's a trick," Monet hissed.

"Maybe its appearance depends on who stares at it," Ever said, approaching the door and turning to face the group. "Tell me what you each see."

Azure answered first. "I see a long hallway with tall columns, mosaic floors, and a golden sarcophagus on the far wall."

"I see a door but kind of can see past it, and also not really," Manx said, squinting.

"Hallway," Monet answered at once.

Laurel scratched her head, confused. "I only see a door."

Ever turned and looked at the entryway. "I see everything that Azure does, as well as the door."

"So what does that mean? Laurel can't see it, Manx kind of can, and the three of us can totally see the hallway," Azure mused, and then she knew. She held her hand out and pushed it through the door, not meeting any obstacles. "Those with magic can pass. Those with little or none cannot."

"Those are my thoughts too," Ever said, extending his own hand.

"I have magic," Manx complained, walking forward. His

head hit the door first, and while he wasn't blocked from passing, it was like he had rammed into a soft pillow. He moved backward, sat on his hind legs, and looked offended.

"You have magic, but it's limited to your shapeshifting. I'm guessing you could pass if you wanted to, but it might take some effort," Azure said.

"And I can't pass at all." Laurel's voice was dejected, and her face spoke of her feelings at being left out.

"It's how these witches guard against vampires and other creatures that might mean them harm. Those without magic can't pass into their headquarters." Azure sank down and picked up Manx, then stepped forward and held the cat out to Laurel. "I'm sorry you can't accompany us, Laurel, but would you two please look after each other?"

Laurel took the pooka a bit begrudgingly. "I wish Nenet would have mentioned this before dragging us all out here."

"I'm sure she wasn't quite thinking clearly, as none of us would have been in her position," Azure said.

Manx changed into a large black dog and Laurel nearly fell backward from the weight of the giant animal. She dropped him at once. "Damn it! You're a jerk."

He wagged his tail and barked delightedly at her. "Oh, come on. I thought that was funny. Why don't we race back to the hotel? Whoever arrives there first gets the first shot of Monet's centaur vodka."

"Don't touch my stash, Dog Bone," Monet warned.

Azure shook her head. "We'll return to the hotel as soon as we can. Please keep an eye out for Finswick. And I want both of you to be careful. Since it's night, vampires could be prowling the streets. Stick together."

The dog and the werecat nodded, and Azure turned her attention to the barrier. She gave Ever, who stood to one side of her, a tentative look. "Are you ready—"

Monet grabbed her wrist and strolled forward. "Come on, Queeny. Let's make some new friends."

13

A melodic trickling sound echoed throughout the long hallway from the fountains next to each of the red columns. The passage was dark, since the only light came from the large fire basins on the far side of the room. The ceiling was riddled with skylights which would light the space during the day.

At the far end of the hallway, the golden sarcophagus sat flush against the wall. There were no doors or other outlets.

"What do you suppose we're to do?" Azure asked, wand out and eyes scanning the space.

"Your new friend Nenet has a horrible reputation already for leaving out pertinent details," Monet said, earning a nod from Ever. The Light Elf looked as perplexed as Azure.

"Well, we know one must have magic to come this far, so it stands to reason that we need to use magic to get any farther into the headquarters," Azure said, thinking aloud.

She strode over to the sarcophagus, which had been detailed very much like the head on the Sphinx they were currently underneath. She gripped her wand and tried a few different spells, but none of them had an effect.

"Queen Azure, why don't you try a simple opening spell?" a voice said at their backs. All three wheeled around to find a girl who looked remarkably like Nenet staring back at them. She had the same brownish-black hair and olive-green eyes, but this girl still had the tattoos.

"Nenet?" Azure asked, peering at her with fear but also interest. Had the vampire come back? Were they safe?

The girl shook her head and hurried forward, picking up her long white robes. "No, but I see you've met my twin sister. I'm Nefertiti."

"Oh. How did you guess that I am Queen Azure?"

"Well, few dress in Victorian gowns in New Egypt since the heat doesn't allow for such things," Nefertiti said, scanning Ever and then Monet briefly.

Azure suddenly felt dumb for wearing such a dress. Shortsighted. "Yes, well, you're right. My gran is not the practical type, and she all but forced me into the dress."

Nefertiti, who was somehow more beautiful than her vampire sister, narrowed her eyes at Azure, a smug look on her pink mouth. "And here I thought you were queen and able to make your own decisions. You should at the very least be able to dress yourself."

"I am." Azure snapped the two words, her cheeks flushing pink. Then she remembered about Nenet. This was her twin, and she'd have to break the news to her. Shoving away her ego, she inclined her head to the door. "You said a simple opening spell would work?"

"Yes, but where is my sister? I suppose she found you," Nefertiti said, looking around.

"She did, and led us here to the Sphinx. Nenet told us to speak with Chibale," Azure said, trying to determine how she could break such devastating news to this girl. Nenet was her twin, and now she was lost to her forever. It wasn't right. But she didn't know how to say what she must, so instead Azure said, "Will you lead us through and introduce us?"

Nefertiti considered her for a moment and then nodded. "Follow me," she said, flicking her wand at the sarcophagus and muttering, "*Patentibus.*"

The wall behind the sarcophagus shook. Azure had expected the chest to slide out of the way, but instead the wall split behind it and receded. Nefertiti strolled through the resulting door, her chin in the air and her hands clasped in front of her.

The commotion in the next room was a stark contrast to the quiet solitude of the hallway. Witches and wizards in flowing white robes lounged around a pool of water that ran the length of the great room. A tall fountain graced the middle of the atrium-like room, trickling water hovering in arcs over the surface. Most people were talking excitedly when the group entered, but all stopped conversing after laying their eyes on the three foreigners.

"Good thinking, wearing the red dress. You stand out like a bloody thumb," Monet said, hardly parting his lips.

"You're one to talk, Green-hair McGoo-head," Azure said. It was an old nickname that she hadn't used for Monet in quite some time. Her nervousness must have brought it to mind.

A man with a group of witches and wizards gathered around him parted from the crowd and hurried over to them. He wore a white linen button-up shirt and his loose-fitting pants matched. His long black hair had been pulled back in a ponytail, and his bright blue eyes were curiously fixed on the group of three. Symbolic tattoos covered the man's hands, arms, chest, neck, and half his face. He looked neither old nor young, but absolutely had a sophisticated attractiveness that gave Azure pause. This man, with his exotic appearance and the trusting eyes, was unlike anyone she'd ever seen. He had a rare grace.

"Nefertiti, thank you for escorting the queen here, but I did ask your sister to do that," the man said.

"I just allowed them into this room. Nenet brought them here, but I don't know where she is," the young witch said.

The man smiled at Azure, a knowing expression in his eyes. "Queen Azure, may we please start with introductions, and then you can fill us in before we do the same."

He extended his tattooed hand. Azure had never seen so many designs on a person. Looking over the man's shoulder, she noted that everyone in the large room was covered in tattoos. The bare legs of the women wading in the long pool were marked, although most people's arms were covered so she couldn't see them. However, no one had any markings on their face, unlike the man before her.

She took his hand and shook it.

"My name is Chibale and I welcome you to New Egypt, although I wish it were under better circumstances."

Azure's smile dropped. "You are a member of the council, aren't you? My tour was made known to you?"

Chibale nodded, pointing to a narrow passage off the main room. "Will you follow me? There's much for us to discuss, and I sense you will not want others around for what you must disclose."

Did he know about Nenet? It seemed like he knew something. "Of course, but first… These gentlemen are members of my cabinet, Monet and Ever." She presented the man on either side of her to Chibale.

"Ah, yes…Monet Torrance. The news of your work with potions has traveled far and wide. I was glad to hear that you'd be accompanying the queen. We could use your expertise, if you wish to converse with our Potion Masters." When he looked at Ever he simply smiled and nodded, but there was something under it, as if he didn't trust the Light Elf.

Azure followed when Chibale turned and strode down the long hallway. The walls sparkled with blue tiles, and the gold under their feet and above their heads made them feel as if they were walking on the beaches of the river.

"You must forgive me, Queen Azure. You know by now that New Egypt is being overrun by vampires. I knew of it when you sent your announcement of the tour, and I knowingly allowed you to enter the city without telling you or your cabinet about it," Chibale disclosed, but there was no guilt on his tattooed face.

"You knew that my cabinet would never allow me in the kingdom if there were vampires roaming about, didn't you?" Azure asked, not yet mad. Maybe this wasn't something to be upset about. She hadn't decided yet.

"I did, but I also knew that we needed alliances. Strong and powerful ones, although that presents a double-edged sword now. I know what you did to save your people from the virus they were infected with by the Land of Terran," Chibale said.

"I have forgiven the people of Terran and we have peaceful relations now. My brother is one of my closest allies," Azure said proudly.

"I understand that. I'm merely speaking of your reputation for overcoming the odds."

"If you wanted my help, why didn't you just ask for it?" Azure said.

"I know of no witch or wizard or other magical species who will run to help a society that's being picked off by vampires. We are helpless against founders, and followers present other threats. For this reason, we've kept the danger a secret from those outside our borders." His eyes swiveled to the ruby gem around her neck, interest growing in his gaze.

"I'm not like others, nor are my people. We are all Oricerans, and will fight to help our people wherever they are," Azure said, meaning it.

"I'd heard about your devotion, but now I see it isn't simply rumor," Chibale said. "The truth is that the river speaks to us, telling us secrets. It has spoken your name many times in connection with our current vampire problem. I knew I must allow you to come to New Egypt, but I had to wait until you arrived to disclose why. Now I realize that the river was right. You're already a part of the solution."

"Why would you say that? I've done nothing to help since I've been here." Azure thought of Nenet and a pang of guilt hit her. Maybe she'd actually done something to *hinder* by getting Nenet bitten. The witch had been there to meet her, after all.

The two leaders strolled down the long corridor shoulder to shoulder, Chibale with his hands clasped behind his back. Monet and Ever were directly behind them, eyes down and ears listening intently. "I know that the river was correct because you've been given something that none of us own and all wish to possess. That necklace... Where did you get it?"

Azure's hands clasped the stone on her chest. At first she wanted to say it was her soul stone, but then she remembered the truth. "A witch in a shop gave it to me. She said it fit, and that it was from Mage Lenore."

Chibale nodded like this all made perfect sense. "You've been chosen, then."

Azure stopped. "Chosen for what?"

"To protect. That necklace is the only one in existence, and it protects the wearer from being bitten by a founder or follower vampire."

"Wait, Azure is immune?" Ever asked, his voice laced with disbelief.

Chibale nodded. "She is." He reached out, fingers inches away from the necklace and eyes curious. Azure froze, unsure if she should pull away or stand still in an act of trust. She closed her fists and remained unmoving. The wizard lifted his blue eyes, a smile in them as he looked at her. "Mage Lenore must have great faith in you."

"Is it true that you found her home on the Mountain of Truth?" a voice asked from the stone floor. Azure peered down to find a sleek black cat with large pointy black ears staring up at her. The feline wore a thick gold collar that resembled a snake and she'd seemingly appeared from nowhere, as cats were wont to do.

"We found Mage Lenore's house," she said, looking at the cat.

"Then you are the first and only witch to meet her in over a century." The animal looked up at Chibale, a blank expression on its face. "The river might be right about her one day replacing the great mage."

The wizard's cheek twitched ever so slightly, but the reaction had been there. The cat had said too much. "This is my familiar, Cleo. She is very, very old and some say a bit senile."

Chibale walked on, and Azure followed at once. They soon came to a round room with stone bas-reliefs of the Egyptian god Anubis, stood around the space. The figures were all caryatids, and they held up the intricate crown molding that graced the room. The ceiling was a dome, painted with a cloudy blue sky. In the middle of the room sat a throne covered in Egyptian hieroglyphics. Azure was not surprised when Chibale took a seat in the throne and looked at her with a noble expression. "Would you like to tell me about Nenet now? I fear it is bad news."

Azure gulped. "I'm afraid you're correct. We found her tonight next to my carriage. She'd been bitten by a founder."

If Chibale was shocked, his face didn't show it. His expression remained stony, as if he were one of the men with jackal heads lining the room. "Nenet was waiting for me when a founder bit her. We gave her animal blood, and she brought us here. I tried to get her to stay and told her we could help her fight the craving, but she said she'd been summoned. Before I could—"

"You cannot battle the dominance a founder has over a follower. We have tried," Chibale said coolly, crossing one leg over the other. His pants rose to show more tattoos on his legs and feet. "Now, did I hear correctly? That you tried to take care of Nenet after she'd been bitten?"

"We told her it was a daft idea, but Azure likes to get herself into mischief. It's part of her charm." Monet was at her side and he tilted his head as he looked at her affectionately. "You're just not happy if you're not giving one of us a heart attack by doing something dumb, are you?" He chipped his fist playfully at her jaw.

"I couldn't leave her there. I thought we could save her somehow. This was my first time with a vampire," Azure said to Chibale, trying to defend her actions.

"Your instincts proved useful because you couldn't be harmed. Not while wearing the necklace," Chibale said.

Azure looked around for a seat or something else, but there was only the one throne in the round room. It felt strange to stand idly while this king sat staring regally at them. She had never liked her own throne and refused to sit in it, but now she recognized how it put those standing in a subservient position. She held up her wand and circled it three times. Before the king, three chairs almost identical to his sprang from the floor.

"You don't mind, do you?" she asked Chibale. "I've been on my feet all night, and unfortunately my gran doesn't think I should wear practical shoes on this trip—only things that will make me twist my ankles."

Chibale slid his eyes to the side with an air of calm superiority. "I guess not," he said mildly.

Azure took a seat, but Ever remained standing while Monet strolled around the room, eyeing the walls. From the entrance, Cleo watched the group, her yellow eyes studying them.

"Will you tell me about your coven? I'm really intrigued by your people. You do not dislodge a soul stone, is that right?" Azure hadn't seen a single witch or wizard with a purple amethyst like the one fastened into the leather band around Monet's wrist.

"That's correct. I understand that each coven is different in that way, somehow dictated by the energy of Oriceran in their geographical homeland. Here in New Egypt, when a witch or wizard comes into power the magic draws the first tattoo on their body, usually on the fingertips or hand."

Chibale tapped his fingers rhythmically on the arm of the chair. Each was covered in symbols from the tip to the second knuckle. The top of his hand had larger streaked designs that circled until they met the wrists. Different artwork covered his arms and shoulders, most of it symbols or patterns. Even more intricate patterns that ran over his chest peeked from his shirt. Tattoos had been drawn on his neck and his face, and the leg that was exposed by his pants riding up had a cast of black ink that ran all the way to his toes.

"Did it hurt?" Monet asked, his tone curious but his eyes on a set of drawings engraved on the wall.

"Did it hurt when you dislodged your soul stone?" Chibale countered.

"It felt like I was choking and going to die, so sure—it hurt a bit," Monet said.

"When magic presents itself from the body or on it, there is displeasure. It's impossible for such a power to not disturb us." Chibale snapped his fingers at Cleo and the feline disappeared, understanding his nonverbal message.

"Your tattoos… They spread as you age, is that correct?" It was Ever who asked this question. He hadn't left his spot behind Azure.

Chibale did not look at him when he answered. "Our soul designs expand as our magic does. The greater our power, the more they cover us. Unlike a soul stone, which represents a witch's power *before* coming to her magic, a wizard's soul design represents who they've become after being granted magic.

"You must be quite powerful," Azure observed.

Chibale steepled his fingers in front of him. "The leader of this coven isn't chosen by blood. We learned our lesson from the old pharaohs. Instead, those with the greatest power and the most extensive soul designs takes the throne. It isn't a role we regard lightly since, unlike *your* title, it can easily be lost. I'm constantly challenged for my position as leader."

Azure stood now, peering down at Chibale. "I fought for my crown. It wasn't simply given to me."

"He's trying to get under your skin," Monet said matter-of-factly, calmly strolling to the next set of pictures and turning to the coven leader. "You don't have to play the 'who's wand is bigger' game, Bale. Azure is here to help you. Keep the subtle insults to a minimum or you'll have to answer to me." Monet narrowed his eyes, turning back to closely study the next set of drawings and looking unflustered by the threat he'd just made.

Chibale stood and motioned for Cleo, who had just appeared in the archway, to come forward. "Cleo, would you lead these three to their rooms? I must attend to Nefertiti. I can sense her growing worried about her sister."

"You can sense her?" Azure asked.

"Yes. We are connected, just as a tributary is connected to the river and it is connected to everything else." Chibale strode for the exit.

"But I have more questions. More things to ask you." Azure was annoyed by the pompous attitude of the King.

Chibale halted, but turned only his head to answer. "And I have more things to tell you. I offer you a place to stay, since the night is still upon us. *You* are safe to travel to your hotel, but your companions are not. In the morning I will explain what we have failed to cover tonight."

"My fucking vodka is at the hotel," Monet said, taking a flask from his robe's pocket and unscrewing the lid.

"What do you call that?" Azure asked as they strode behind the feline, who had her tail high in the air. She thought about Finswick, wondering where he was. He'd be fine. He always was, but she wished he were here to insult this cat. Tell her that her collar was on too tight, based on the smug look on her face. Maybe she was being too uptight about this coven. They were going through a hard time. It was just that she wasn't sure if they could be trusted, although at first she'd been well disposed toward Chibale. *They are just different,* she told herself. *Different isn't bad.*

"I call this 'not enough,'" Monet said, shaking the flask. The liquor swished back and forth.

Ever grabbed Azure's arm and pulled her to a halt. "We don't have to stay here tonight. We could send a message to

Oak and have him bring the carriage, or we could just leave now on our own."

"You won't make it far," Cleo said. She had paused as well, and turned her head over her shoulder.

"I think you underestimate our carriage and its coachman, Litter Box," Monet said to the feline.

"Maybe I do, but you still have to get into and out of it, which is when you can expect to be hunted by a vampire. They prowl viciously at night. And if I'm not mistaken, you are Monet Torrance, the powerful Potions Master. They will want *you*. A founder would no doubt take you," Cleo said, batting her long eyelashes.

"And what about Ever?" Monet asked, sounding curious.

"What about the Light Elf? I suppose followers have to feed," the cat said, facing them and sitting down.

Azure blinked surprised by the cat's rude remark. She'd noticed since the beginning the standoffish way they had treated Ever. Were they intolerant of other species? Maybe they didn't trust him because he wasn't a witch or wizard. Their barriers did keep out those without magic, but he'd gotten around that by being a Light Elf.

"Ever, I can't risk something happening to you or Monet. I'll send word to Laurel that we're all right and staying over. Let's meet with Chibale first thing in the morning, and then we'll decide what to do next." Before Azure could say another word, Cleo rose and started strolling down the long corridor again. They followed her back to the main room and then to another hallway through another doorway.

"The queen is in the first room, and her servants are in

the following two," Cleo said, continuing past the three sets of doors.

"I'm not her servant," Monet scoffed.

"I believe you were introduced as her cabinet members, which makes you her servants," the cat said before disappearing around a corner.

Azure paused, her hand on the doorknob. "Don't let her get to you. We're a team, and you both know it." Azure realized how tired she was just then, and waved a polite goodnight to the guys as she entered her room.

In the morning Azure was awakened by a soft rapping on the door. At least, she thought it was morning. There were no windows in the small round room with its potted tropical plants and tapestries. Having no natural light was one of the downfalls of living under the Sphinx, she supposed. The plants must have been enchanted with a sunshine spell in order to grow and stay alive.

"What?" she groaned, realizing she'd only slept a few hours. It had taken longer than she liked to write a message to Laurel on a piece of parchment and enchant it to fly as a paper airplane to its recipient. She'd mastered that easy spell long ago, but her magic worked differently here for some reason. Or maybe it was the necklace. Whatever it was, the long night had left her exhausted. She'd need one of those potions Monet made that kept him going on days when he stayed up late drinking.

The door to her room opened and Nefertiti's head

popped through. Her hair had been braided into three separate sections, each with gold strung through it.

"Oh…Nefertiti," Azure said. She bolted up, then realized she only had on her undergarments. She pulled the crisp linen sheet around her to shield herself. She'd found it impossible to sleep in the tight red dress, and had decided it was safe to take it off for the night. Now it was strewn on the chair on the far side of the small room. "I'm so sorry about Nenet. You know by now, don't you?"

"I'm sorry too," Nefertiti said, coming into the room and closing the door behind her. She held a stack of linens in her hands and wore a calm expression on her face. "I knew that Nenet would end up getting herself bitten. She was always taking unnecessary risks."

Azure tensed, studying the girl. "You don't seem as heartbroken as I thought you'd be. Are you in shock?"

"I'm pissed," Nefertiti said, venom in her voice. "We'll discuss that in a minute. First, take these clothes. They aren't the tight-fitting gowns you're used to, but they are better-suited for the heat of the desert, and they're clean."

Azure didn't hesitate. She'd much rather be practical than fashionable. And she had quite liked the draped white clothes the witches of New Egypt wore.

"Oh, I forgot your sandals," Nefertiti said. She pulled a bronze wand from a pocket of her dress. It looked somewhat like Azure's, but had a hook at the top, like the crook that was often seen with sarcophagi. Crook and flail, Azure remembered from her lessons. The crook represented power, and the flail the abundance of the land. When Nefertiti pointed it into the air, a pair of leather sandals of a minimalistic design appeared on the floor before her feet.

At once Azure's eyes swelled with gratitude. "Practical shoes! Thank you."

Nefertiti turned her back, directing her eyes to the far wall. "Get dressed and I'll show you to the dining hall. Chibale waits for you there."

Azure pulled the white gown over her head. It was as light as silk, but felt durable and strong. It hooked over one shoulder, leaving the other bare, and the rest of the cloth flowed to the ground. She slipped on the sandals and checked her appearance in the mirror.

Before she could say she was ready, Nefertiti spun back. Her eyes barely grazed Azure before she headed for the door. She halted there and turned back, her olive-green eyes overflowing with tears suddenly. "I'm heartbroken that my sister has been turned. I've seen it happen to a few, but now this is personal. Chibale says the river whispers your name for a reason. Queen Azure, please help us. You may not be able to save my sister, but you *must* help save my people, if for no other reason than my sister and others like her. She was a good person. More good people will be turned if the vampires are allowed to reign."

Azure couldn't find her voice for a moment. Being face to face with a stranger's pain wasn't easy. She didn't take the fact that this girl and these witches needed her help lightly, but she had no idea how to fix any of this or why Mage Lenore had the necklace given to her. After a moment she shook her head. "I'll do everything that I can. I promise you that much."

"I trust that you will," Nefertiti said, opening the door. "I would prefer that my people do not see me in this way. Will you show yourself to breakfast?"

The girl's eyes were wet, her eyelashes clumped together with tears. Aside from that she looked the perfect picture of poise. Still, Azure nodded.

"The dining area is down this hallway on the left. You can't miss it. Chibale has the long table in the center reserved for you all. You are to sit at the far end of the table, and do not eat until he does. It is a show of respect for your host," Nefertiti said and then she was gone, scurrying down the hallway in the opposite direction.

Azure smoothed down the hair around her braid as she headed out of her room. The hallway was empty and was lit by torches like most of the areas she'd been in. She heard trickling water, and was unsurprised to find a round fountain with three levels when she turned the corner. It sat at the far end of the hallway, with outlets on either side. The New Egyptians seemed to enjoy fountains, which she found quite interesting. It must have been the connection to the river.

To the left she heard the clinking of plates and conversations, so that was where the dining hall was. She turned briefly to see what was in the opposite hallway and a bright light nearly blinded her. Azure held up her arm in self-defense, but soon realized that she wasn't in immediate danger. She brought her arm down, thinking she'd see a reflective light of some sort that had been bounced off a plate of metal, but what she found wasn't something she could describe. It wasn't a reflection, but rather a sliver of light hanging in the open space of the hallway.

Tentatively Azure approached the light, which was a few inches wide in the middle and tapered at the ends. She moved close to it and then stepped past it, thinking it was coming from something on the other side. It wasn't, and it disappeared when she went behind it. She stepped back, and there was the light again. And now she could see something moving in it. Were those faces? She squinted. There was definitely something in there, but what was it?"

"I was afraid you'd gotten lost," Ever said at her back, nearly making her lose her breath.

Azure started and spun. The Light Elf stood in the arch leading to the dining hall wearing a white button-up shirt and linen pants similar to those Chibale had worn the day before.

"Oh, I'm glad you're here. Look, what is this?" She turned around and the sliver of light was gone. It had disappeared.

"What is what?" Ever asked.

Azure whipped around. "You didn't see it when you came up? There was a light."

"A light? Like what kind of light?" he asked, sounding interested.

"I don't know. At first it was blinding and then I thought I saw something in it, like people, but now it's gone."

Ever nodded, not an ounce of skepticism in his expression. "Maybe Chibale will know and can explain. He's waiting for you. Are you ready?"

"Yes," Azure said at once, strolling forward but still slightly unnerved by the strange light. "I'm anxious to get answers and return to our group. I don't like leaving the others out there without us."

"I agree," Ever said, calmly striding beside her.

The dining hall was filled with small round tables, and witches and wizards had gathered around them to share their breakfasts. In the center was a twelve-person rectangular table with Chibale at one end. Azure stared at the other end, which seemed so far from her host when they had important matters to talk about. Monet sat on one side, and the rest of the chairs were empty.

Fuck customs, Azure thought, taking the seat next to Chibale. They needed to speak, and screaming over five place settings would just be ridiculous.

Chibale tightened his eyes at Azure, his displeasure at her not following their rules evident.

"Last night you said that my being in New Egypt was a double-edged sword. What did you mean by that?" She launched straight into her most burning question while picking up a piece of the flat bread from the middle of the table and spreading orange jelly on it. She hadn't realized how hungry she was until she'd smelled the baked fruit and roasted meats in the dining hall.

Chibale rotated his head slightly and peered at her as if wondering what she'd do next. She eyed his untouched plate of food. Azure tore off a piece of the bread and popped it into her mouth, then dropped the rest onto her plate.

"Queen Azure, you aren't like any nobility I've ever met," Chibale said sternly, fingers tightening around his brass goblet.

"Is that a problem?" Azure asked. "I can only be who I am."

Chibale's mouth flattened into a hard line and his eyes bounced around on her features. Suddenly he broke into a loud laugh. "Not a problem for me. You might actually be a real person after all." He raised his goblet ,which gained the attention of everyone in the dining hall. "Please join me in welcoming our newest ally, and the most remarkable queen I've ever had the pleasure of dining with. Queen Azure, the New Egyptians welcome you. Our home is yours. Our kingdom awaits your grace. Glory to the queen of Virgo!"

There was a great stir in the dining hall as people picked up their goblets and lifted them. "Glory to the queen," they toasted in unison.

Azure gazed at the faces. Some had tattoos, but most wore only smiles.

"Thank you, Chibale. I realize now I was being tested," Azure said boldly to the king.

"Isn't everything a test?" he asked seriously.

"I guess it's about perspective." Azure took a steaming bowl of eggs and ladled some onto her plate.

"Back to your question, Queen Azure. Yes, your being here is a double-edged sword, as I mentioned last night. I need resources to fight these vampires, since I'm struggling alone, and I believe you would be a strong ally. However, what this coven of vampires wants is strong witches and wizards to turn. We've lost some of our best to them already. I'm certain that they would want to make you and me into founders." Chibale leaned forward, his blue eyes burning with frustration. "I don't know enough, and what I *do* know only begs more questions."

"Let's start with what you know," Azure said between bites.

"I believe that New Egypt was chosen by this coven for a reason. Egypt, on Earth, is where the first vampire was created. The pharaohs on Earth employed wizards to build the pyramids and the Sphinx. It was then that a bat came upon a wizard casting magic, and a vampire was born. The bats are attracted to the magic and absorb it, becoming one with the witch or wizard. That's how founders are created. Followers are born when a founder bites another. Ra, the God of the Sun, cursed vampires to be unable to walk during the day. There was a battle between the gods, and Osiris rose and made vampires immortal. Vampires acquired their powers in Egypt. Egypt on both Earth and Oriceran is where vampires are strongest, but also weakest because of how the gods control them. That is as much as I know. Like I said, this information only raises more questions."

"So if vampires were born in Egypt, then it stands to reason that their undoing resides there as well," Ever said from his place beside Azure.

Chibale stroked his chin, musing on the idea. "That's a hopeful thought, but maybe a bit too optimistic."

"What's the connection between your Egypt and the one on Earth?" Monet asked, filling his goblet.

"They are twin kingdoms, very much like Nenet and Nefertiti are twins," Chibale explained.

"You mean that they look the same mostly but there are inherent differences, right?" Azure asked.

"Exactly. There's energy bleeding between our world and Earth, and it started in Egypt. The crystal on top of the

Great Pyramid helps resonate the magical energy on Earth. It was created to siphon energy between portals on Earth and Oriceran," Chibale said.

A chill ran down Azure's back, making her shiver, but she wasn't sure why.

Chibale paused at her reaction. "Are you all right?"

"Yes," she said at once, her head buzzing with questions. "This energy siphon... Is that why the cities mirror each other?"

"That's exactly why. These are parallel universes. The pyramids were created on Earth, but what is constructed there becomes tangible here and vice versa. However, over time the things created change. The magic on Oriceran preserves things, in a way," Chibale said.

"Is it possible that there are natural portals between our world and Earth, and they present themselves in New Egypt? Like holes or tears between the worlds due to this siphoned energy?" Azure asked, thinking of the strange light she saw earlier in the hallway.

Chibale pushed out his chair and stood suddenly, leaning over Azure with a strange intensity in his eyes. "Have you seen one of the holes?"

Azure bristled at his sudden reaction. "Yes, I think so—earlier in the hallway. Why?"

"The river spoke of these tears recently. It told our people that answers to the vampires could be found on the other side of one of these. We've searched the kingdom and never found one. Where was it?" Chibale straightened, peering at the hallway she'd come in from.

"It's gone now. So you're saying it's in Egypt? We need

to go to Earth-Egypt?" Azure turned to Ever. "Can you create a portal to there?"

He shook his head. "I've never understood why until now, but I can't create portals to Egypt."

"That's because the only way directly there is through one of these tears. Queen Azure, you must find a tear again and travel through it. This is the most hope we've had in quite some time." Chibale's expression was a mix of anxious worry and excitement. He was vibrating with it.

"Easy-peasy. Azure, we need you to walk around New Egypt until you find a tiny tear in the world. That shouldn't take long," Monet drawled, leaning back in his chair with his goblet in hand.

Chibale turned slowly and looked at him. "She's the only one who has seen a tear. Maybe it's the necklace. Whatever the reason, we need to find the tear again and go through."

"Maybe there's another solution." Azure felt around and realized that she had left her bag in her room. "I have a genie's lamp. Maybe I can have him—"

"You have a what?" Chibale cut her off, somehow mustering even more astonishment.

"A genie's lamp. We found it on our way here," Azure said, standing as well. She was tired of Chibale leaning over her.

"That's simply incredible. No lamp has returned to New Egypt in quite some time," he said.

"Bob, the genie… He's afraid of New Egypt. Can you tell me more about the lamp's history?" Azure asked.

"I can, but not now. It's a very sordid tale, and will take much longer than we have. But don't waste a wish on trying to find a tear. By the time you get there it could be gone, and then you'd be down one wish," Chibale advised.

"Okay, so back to strolling around the desert willy-nilly. Good plan." Monet stood, swaying slightly as if his feet had gone to sleep while he sat.

"I wish there was another way, Queen Azure, but this is our best chance. My people are relying on you," Chibale said.

Monet had already come around the table and hooked his arm through Azure's. "Let's stroll around and find this tear between the universes. My flask is newly filled, so we'll get drunk while we do it."

15

Azure stopped at her room to get her bag, which contained the lamp. She couldn't believe she'd left it behind; such a treasure really shouldn't be forgotten. What if someone had stolen it? She strapped the bag over her shoulder and set out to find the tear.

"Where do we go first?" Monet asked, handing his flask to her. Ever had returned to the hotel to check on Laurel and Manx, although Azure also thought it was to get away from the witches and wizards here. They all gave him strange looks and treated him as an outsider.

"I saw the tear in the hallway next to the dining hall, so let's go in that direction." Azure set off for the hallway with the giant fountain and scanned for the bright light as they walked.

"What do you make of this Chibale character?" Monet asked, pulling a package from his robes.

"What's that?" Azure asked, taking a small sip from the

flask. It was a bit too early to be drinking, but searching for a mysterious break between universes to find unknown information on stopping vampires was definitely a reason to break the rules.

Monet opened the wrapper to reveal a piece of yellow candy. "It's Laffy Taffy. I scored a whole bag of Earth candy in the Dark Market for this trip." He took a bite from the stubborn piece of candy, stretching it to three times its normal length. After chewing a great deal he grimaced. "Gross—it's banana-flavored. Why would anyone ever make something banana-flavored?" Reluctantly he swallowed, a sour look on his face the whole time.

"To answer your question, I think I trust Chibale. I think he's governed by certain traditions, and maybe he's a bit closed-minded about those who aren't witches and wizards—like Ever—but he seems to be a strong leader. I couldn't imagine if our people were being hunted by vampires," Azure said, turning to scan the hallway they'd just come through.

"Oh, you couldn't imagine your people losing their magic due to a deadly virus?" Monet mocked.

"Okay, well, I guess I could." Azure laughed. "I still wonder why Mage Lenore intended for me to have this necklace. And why can I see the tears?"

"All curious questions which I'm sure we won't find out for three more books," Monet said, unwrapping another Laffy Taffy.

"What are you talking about? Are you drunk?"

"Why, yes I am. Do you ever think that we're just characters in a book and there's this author person writing our story? I bet the readers love the hell out of me." Monet's cheeks were pink from the alcohol.

"You've lost your damn mind. I'm certain that if our story were in a book everyone would want you dead." Azure looked at the ceiling. "Author person, if you exist and are writing our story, will you please kill Monet in the next act?"

He shook his head as he read the wrapper. "Hey, this candy is going to break my teeth, but on the bright side there are jokes in the wrappers. Listen to this one." Monet cleared his throat. "Why is a bad joke like a bad pencil?"

"I don't know," Azure answered as they approached a new set of rooms.

"Because it has no point!" Monet gave a fake laugh and slapped his thigh.

"Ha, ha." Azure paused when they entered a large space that reminded her of the greenhouses in Virgo. Palm trees lined the walls, almost hiding them, and the floor changed suddenly. It was covered in dirt, and plants had been scattered everywhere. A path snaked around the room.

"Uh, did we just step outside? I thought we were underground," Monet said, looking up from the new piece of candy he'd just opened.

"We are, but I think this is where they grow their plants and herbs," Azure said, looking up. There was a strange source of light that resembled the sun.

"Hmmm. I should probably investigate some of their native plants to see what properties they have," Monet said, still chewing on the candy.

"You're supposed to be helping me find a rift between worlds, remember?"

"That's boring. I've decided to provide the entertainment instead. Okay, new joke time." Monet held up a wrapper and read. "When do you stop at a green and go at a red?"

Azure strolled along the path, searching everywhere. "I have no idea."

"When you're eating a watermelon…" Monet said, his voice trailing off.

"I don't get it."

"Yeah, me either. Must be an Earth thing."

"Speaking of Earth, I wonder what is in their Egypt that will help with the vampires," Azure mused, peeking around a tree at more of the tropical garden.

"Beats me. Maybe a stake? That's how you kill vampires, right?"

"Actually that's a myth." Something suddenly occurred to her, and she wasn't sure why she hadn't thought about it earlier. Azure dug into her bag until she found the knife that Drago the orc had given her. "The orcs were pivotal in hunting the vampires when they took over a century ago. It was something about the way they forged their weapons that made them so successful. The metal they use for their blades was unique to them, and apparently deadly to vampires."

"And conveniently you have an orc knife." Monet looked up at the ceiling. "A bit *too* convenient, storyteller."

"Oh, shut it. This knife has saved your ass a bunch of times." Azure pushed it into Monet's hands along with the flask. "I want you to take this. That way, if you run into any vampires you can defend yourself."

"And what about you?" Monet asked, taking the flask but pushing the knife back in her direction.

She turned and walked farther away, not taking the weapon. "I've got a magical necklace, remember?"

"Fine, fine, I'll take your knife." Monet stuck the knife in the inside pocket of his robe.

Azure stepped off the path toward a strange red flower. It had thorns on the petals, something she'd never seen before. Usually the petals were soft and the thorns were on the stem.

"That's an interesting flower," she said, pointing.

"What's that?" Monet asked.

She turned to him, but was blinded by a light behind him. Instantly she pulled up her arm to shield her eyes.

"You okay?" Monet asked.

Azure lowered her arm, realizing at once what the light was from. It was still bright but it wasn't too much, only at first glance. "Monet, behind you! There's a tear!"

Monet wheeled around, full of excitement, and then deflated completely. "How much centaur vodka did you drink?"

"Look, it's right there." She pointed directly at the tear. This one was wider than the one she had seen in the hallway. It hung in the air. On the other side was mostly darkness, but a structure of some sort was visible—maybe a column?

"Are you fucking with me? I don't see a damn thing," Monet said.

"No, are you fucking with me? It's here." Azure strode forward and put her hand through the tear. It was warm on the other side, the air stuffy as if there were no ventilation.

"Oh, fuck me! That's gnarly." Monet's mouth hung open.

"What?" Azure asked, pulling her hand back.

"Your hand disappeared. You've really found a tear, haven't you?"

"Yes, but I'm not sure how long it will be here. We need to go through before it disappears like the other one," Azure said, sticking her hand through the opening again.

"Unfortunately, love, I think you're on your own. If I can't see the tear, then my guess is I can't go through it," Monet said, waving his hand where hers was. It stayed visible.

"Damn it! I have to go alone? What the hell?" Azure wasn't sure what she'd find on the other side. Worse, she didn't know where she'd be. It looked dark. And how would she get back to New Egypt? She'd have to find another tear.

"You'll be fine. If anyone can do this, it's you." Monet placed a reassuring hand on her shoulder. "I'll go back to the hotel and wait with Ever. If you're not back in a day, we'll open the closest portal we can find and come looking for you."

Azure nodded, grateful that Monet had her back. She wanted to say something else, to arrange more of plan, but there was no time. "Thank you," was all she said before she stuck her arm all the way through the opening. The feel of the air was different from where she was, but she tried not to think of or fear any of that. As if she were slipping between the sheets of a bed Azure slid her body through the opening, picking up her feet to step through the crack.

Her foot came down on a hard surface, much different than the soft ground where she'd been. The last thing she brought through was her head, and the last thing she saw was Monet staring at her with hesitation on his face. She looked around her new location and saw only blackness.

16

It took several seconds for Azure's eyes to adjust to the dark room. She stayed completely frozen, taking in the smells, sights, and sounds around her. The air was dank with dust and it was warm, so warm that Azure was already sweating. And there wasn't a single noise, which made her feel deaf. She turned back to the tear between the worlds, but it had vanished. *Of course it was gone,* she thought. She'd have to find a different way back.

Lifting her wand, she said, *"Illustrant."* The tip of the wand lit and Azure suddenly backed up three giant steps.

A skeleton lay just in front of her. "Of-fucking-course. I had to land in a place with dead bodies."

She turned in a circle, taking in the space. Besides the skeleton, she was alone in this mostly-empty chamber. She couldn't see the ceiling, but had a feeling it was high above her, as those in the chambers under the Sphinx in Oriceran had been. The walls were covered in spider webs, which did nothing to increase her comfort. "Just me and the spiders down here," she whispered to herself.

Down here, she thought. Why did she think she was *down here?* The tear had led her to Egypt, which was parallel to New Egypt. There she'd been under the Sphinx, so it made sense she'd be in the same place on Earth.

Azure backed up to the large square columns. This did seem like a tomb or temple of sorts. What had Chibale said? New Egypt and Egypt were twins, similar yet different. That meant that the way out of this was up ahead, down a narrow corridor. Azure longed to be out of the dark musty prison, so she strode forward and nearly slipped on a slick surface. Lowering her wand, she narrowed her eyes at what had caused her to lose her footing. On the stone ground it was hard to see anything due to the dust, but she made out the faint outline of a piece of parchment. She tentatively picked at the edges until she had a grip. Lifting the parchment, she held her wand to it. There were rows and rows of hieroglyphs. The page was torn on one side, like it had been ripped from a book. *Book,* she thought. Wasn't there a significant book that had belonged to the Egyptians? From seemingly nowhere a title popped into her head. Book of the Dead. She'd heard that before. Could this be from that?

Behind her she heard something shuffling and she spun, wand high. On the other side of the chamber a single black spider the size of her palm crawled out of a corner.

"Fuck, that's a big spider!" she whispered, slightly disgusted. At least there was only the one.

A great scurrying filled the chamber suddenly and Azure backed away from the noise. Black spread on the stone floor behind the single spider, engulfing it. The blackness covered the walls like paint. She guessed the black had overwhelmed the ceiling above too. Azure blinked and then realized that the black was hundreds, maybe thousands of large, menacing spiders. They paused, forming a wall several feet away. "Oh, fuck," she said, stuffing the parchment into her bag. She took another step back and met stone and air. There were stairs behind her.

Without warning, the spiders raced at Azure. She whipped her wand in their direction and shot a bolt of fire at them, hitting the first line. Smoke filled the chamber, which instantly made her eyes burn. She wheeled and raced up the stairs, sprinting in an unknown direction. The skittering of spider legs filled the space behind her but she didn't dare turn around. She could only keep racing forward, although she was unsure what she'd find ahead.

Now she was running blind, having lost the light from the fire. She brought her wand up again and lit it, and immediately halted before running straight into a stone wall. She was stuck—there was no way out. The scuttling grew louder, so loud it hurt her ears. The spiders would be on her any second now. Azure could fight off some of the spiders, but there were too many. Did she have time to get the lamp out of her bag? She didn't think so.

She backed up, expecting to feel stone behind her, but instead she felt nothing. Another step backwards, and still no wall. When Azure turned, she saw a strange light and more steps. But how could that be? Then she remembered the barrier wall beneath the Sphinx in New Egypt. What if that was what this stone door was? An illusion to keep what was in the chamber there and only allow in magical species? Azure took three more steps backward, and to her relief she could now see the stone door in front of her. On the other side were the faint outlines of the hundreds of spiders who had raced to the top of the stairs. They had halted only a few feet away and their angry red eyes stared around, but they couldn't cross the barrier.

Letting out a breath, Azure turned and shielded her eyes. At first she thought she was seeing another tear between the worlds, but then she realized it was moonlight. A warm white light shone at the top of the stairs. Taking the steps two at a time Azure ran to the top, grateful to be outside again and not trapped underground. It had made her feel claustrophobic to be under the Sphinx. She halted at the top, not at all prepared for what she saw next.

The Sphinx on Earth was not at all like the one on Oriceran. It was the same shape and general size, but the painted face of the pharaoh was only one of the differences. The headdress was significantly diminished here on Earth, and the nose had been destroyed. On Oriceran the Sphinx still looked as it had for millennia. This Sphinx had suffered from time, eroded by sand and wind and sun.

Azure was less surprised when she looked at the Great Pyramid and saw the same thing. It was not a pristine structure like the one on Oriceran. This pyramid, even from a distance, was worn and looked like it might crumble away. She hoped desperately that it didn't. Was this what the magic on Oriceran did? Preserved these structures, whereas on Earth they wasted away more each year?

This surprise had stolen Azure's attention, but she soon

realized how cool it was. During the day in the desert the heat was stiflingly oppressive, but at night the cold desert air cloaked her, making her shiver. A single moon hung in the Earth sky, making her long to be back on Oriceran. She had the parchment. That had to be what the river had referred to, or at least it was one of the many clues she needed to fight the vampires.

Another shiver shook her. She needed to get inside, and quickly. Almost as important, she needed to find a way back to Oriceran. Azure spun toward the skyline of the city and sucked in a breath. A man with a bald head and a beard stood inches away. She hadn't even known he was there. He had a large stone in his hand and a wide smile on his face, displaying the sharp fangs prominent in his mouth.

"Well, hello, love! This is gonna hurt a bit." He brought the brick down on her head, and the world went black.

17

The howling pain in the top of Azure's head woke her. She tried to sit up, but realized she couldn't move. She hadn't been bound, but her muscles didn't work. Desperately she tried to twist or turn, but it was impossible. Her limbs were paralyzed, and the realization sent panic through her mind.

She cracked open one eye to find that her face was pressed into a bed, her gaze blurry. Could she blink her eyes? Yes, she had that much control, but that wasn't saying a lot. Her head hurt badly and she tried to groan, but her mouth wouldn't open. It felt as if it were sealed shut. It took several seconds for her to realize that all she could see was a blue blanket under her face.

Tapping. It was the first noise she heard.

"I thought you'd be impressed by what I've brought you, Madam. I was amazed when the queen turned up. I hadn't expected to find her there, and poof! She appeared just as I was trying to find my way into the Sphinx," a voice said.

"You want me to pat you on the head, Lux? You got lucky. And you know there's no way for you to get into the Sphinx, not anymore. It's protected from vampires. We haven't been allowed in there in centuries," a woman's voice said, sounding impatient.

The memories flooded Azure's mind. Coming out of the Sphinx, the vampire, the stone. She'd awakened here among more vampires. Doom crushed her spirit. She was trapped…a prisoner.

"Well, you said there was something important in the Sphinx, so I thought I'd try and find it. What was it again?" the man's voice said. He sounded as if he were desperately trying to impress the woman.

"I didn't say, since we don't know what it is. There are things scattered all over Egypt that can help or hinder us— that's all Ata knows for sure. One of them can be found in the Sphinx, or maybe more than just one clue," the woman said.

"So why don't you send Ata into the Sphinx?" the man asked.

"Because I need him here, and he couldn't see a tear between Oriceran and Earth like we can. They are intended for vampires to use to get between worlds," the woman explained, her voice tight with irritation.

Azure pressed her eyes closed, trying to listen over the pounding in her head.

Tap. Tap. Tap. It was an impatient sound. "This girl, the queen—how did she get to Egypt?" a new person said, this. It was a soft, melodic male voice.

"She's wearing the Mage's Necklace. I'm guessing it gives her vampire sight. It certainly makes her appear as a vampire, which is how she can go unnoticed on the streets by our followers. They don't even smell her. It's as if she's one of them," the woman explained.

"But *you* smell her, don't you?" the first man asked. "I didn't smell her, but I knew who she was based on what you told us about her."

"I can smell her blood, but I can't touch her. Not until we get that damn necklace off her. Ata is working on it. Soon the girl will be vulnerable once more," the woman said.

"Before I opened a tear and brought her back here, I tried to get the necklace off her. It burned my hands...see?" the first man said.

"Lux, I'm tired of looking at you. You were supposed to be on Earth rounding up bats. Get back to your job! I need those to turn this queen into a founder, since the other bats were lost." The woman seemed to blame Lux for losing the bats. She didn't sound pleased with him, however he tried to earn her favor. "Actually, I think Azure's entire entourage will make excellent founders. Our spies say the wizard and Light Elf are very powerful. They couldn't be more perfect," the woman said coolly.

"Yes, Madam. Devo and I have heard rumor of bats in Lancothy, so we'll go there next before returning to Earth." A door opened and footsteps trailed away.

"What is it, Ata?" the woman asked, her voice echoing in the opposite direction.

"The binding spell I put on the girl tells me she's trying to fight it. That means she's awake," another voice said.

A small bit of clapping. "Oh, good news. I've been dying to talk with the little witch," the woman said.

"Good one, Cordelia," the smooth voice of the second man said.

"Sit her up. I'd love to have her looking at us," the woman said.

A second later Azure was whipped onto her back, the act making her head scream. She launched to a sitting position and her eyes sprang open to ascertain what was before her.

The space was similar to her hotel room. She was lying on a stiff bed with tables on either side. The walls were covered in burnt-orange stucco, and large potted palms were scattered here and there. In front of the bed stood a woman with long silky black hair, which was half up and half down. She wore a midnight-blue Victorian dress that trailed behind her, reminding Azure of one of her own stifling garments. The woman was exceptionally beautiful, with porcelain skin and ruby-red lips. Her eyes were curious as they studied Azure, who was still wearing the white gown Nefertiti had given her.

Sitting relaxed in an armchair to the side was a man as attractive as the woman. He had black hair with a silver streak through it, and wore a smart suit as well as an arrogance that screamed he knew something of great importance and refused to share it. In the doorway stood a man who was completely covered in tattoos. Unlike Chibale, whose face was half-covered with tattoos, this man had them all the way to his hairline. Also like Chibale, he had black hair pulled back in a ponytail, and similar blue eyes. He actually looked a great deal like the king of the New Egyptian coven. He wore a loose-fitting black shirt and pants, and a look of pure intolerance.

The woman named Cordelia looked sideways at the wizard. "Ata, allow her to speak, but nothing else."

Ata held up a wand similar to the one Azure had seen Nefertiti use. He waved it, and Azure's lips parted. She hadn't even realized that she had been holding her breath until her mouth popped open and she gasped. The two vampires and the wizard before her had stolen her attention.

"She's a pretty little thing, isn't she?" Cordelia said to the man in the chair. "Just imagine how much more beautiful she'll be once she's been turned."

"I won't be turned. You can't do that. Who are you, and how dare you hold me against my will?" Azure demanded, trying to break free of the binding. The wizard named Ata must have placed her under an enchantment. An incredibly strong one, by the feel of it.

"You're right, we can't. Not as long as you have that little necklace on, but soon Ata will figure out how to remove it," the man in the chair said calmly.

"Where are our manners? We completely skipped introductions. How rude," the woman said, sounding amused. "I'm Cordelia, and this is Hamilton. We are founders who survived the great persecution. After spending a hundred years in hiding, we're ready to rebuild our coven. We've selected you to join us. Isn't that wonderful?"

Azure tried again to break free of the binding charm, but it seemed useless. She'd never encountered magic that was so resistant to her power. In the corner she spied her bag. Her wand was in there, along with the parchment she had found in the Sphinx, but it was useless to her on the other side of the room. And it didn't matter, since she was still frozen. This wizard, based on the number of tattoos he had, must be incredibly powerful. Why was he working for these vampires, Azure wondered?

"Delia my love, I don't think she believes this is wonderful," Hamilton observed, looking quite amused. *Tap. Tap Tap.* He rapped his fingers on the lion head which comprised the arm of the chair.

Cordelia made a dismissive gesture. "Oh, she will. Queen Azure just needs time. Once she's a vampire, she'll love our lifestyle. Our coven will grow strong, with the very best founders in all of history. It will be simply marvelous. There will be no bowing this time. We're going to grow our numbers the right way, and when they come after us it will be too late."

"You're sick. You're the one who turned Nenet, aren't you? You two are attacking New Egypt," Azure said, a sour taste in her mouth. Her head was still throbbing, but right now her anger owned her.

"Guilty as charged," the woman said with a laugh, her fangs showing. They strangely made her more beautiful, and Azure hated that the thought had even occurred to her.

"Ata, how long until you can remove the necklace from the queen?" Hamilton asked.

"I'm not certain. It's appears to be a part of her currently, like it was bound to her with magic," the wizard said, standing stoically in the doorway.

"I expect it to be done by the time Devo and Lux return with more bats. Once Azure is a vampire she'll have no trouble turning her friends," Cordelia said.

"As I mentioned, removing the necklace will be difficult. I will do it, but can make no promises about how long it will take. It shouldn't be long, though," Ata said.

"Oh, fine. Maybe we should turn Azure's friends first. Then she'll have to join them," Cordelia insisted.

"Yes, vampires need forever companions," Hamilton said tapping his fingers on the arm of the chair again.

"We still have one or two bats in storage, correct?" Cordelia asked.

"Yes, but you know that the art of creating a founder isn't precise. It all depends on timing," Hamilton said.

Cordelia whirled and stuck her hands on her hips. She had long red fingernails that matched her lips. "You, Queen Azure, can make this easy or difficult. When the time comes you must perform magic; something simple is fine. The bat will do the rest. If you don't screw it up it will go as planned, and then we don't waste bats." She looked at her companion. "How many did we go through with you, dear?"

Hamilton tapped his fingertips again, thinking. "Too many to count. I admit I was scared, but in the end you were right. Becoming a vampire was the right choice."

Cordelia casually looked at Azure, reaching out her long-nailed hand and nearly touching her cheek. It seemed as though she couldn't actually close the distance, though. Something was preventing the founder from touching her. The necklace, she guessed. "See?" Cordelia said plaintively, like that explained it all and washed away any arguments. "It's all going to be lovely. We'll be one happy coven. Finally vampires will return to the glory that was stolen from us." Cordelia knelt, looking fondly up at Azure. "And it's all going to start with you, my dear. You, your friends, and then your kingdom."

"No!" The word shot out of Azure's mouth so fast it stole her breath.

"Oh, yes," Cordelia said, nodding patiently. These two were too casual, acting as if they were discussing something trivial over afternoon tea. "Virgoans are perfect. And once we have you and your people, taking over the coven in the Sphinx will be easy. We can't touch Chibale yet, but soon. Isn't that right, my darling Ata?"

The wizard nodded, reminding Azure more of a robot than of a man.

"You can't do this," Azure argued, trying again to twist free but remaining as still as Ata.

"Now shush, dear. Don't wear yourself out." Cordelia looked at Hamilton. "I think I should go and fetch her friends. That will make her feel better, don't you think?"

"That's a lovely idea. Just the two, though. I don't want the werecat in here. I loathe cats," Hamilton said, his nose crinkling in disgust.

"I agree, and the pooka is worthless to us as well. I'll just kill those two. It should only take a second," Cordelia said cheerfully.

"No!" Azure screamed again. "They'll fight you. Ever and Monet can't be taken. You'll fail."

Cordelia gave her a pitying smile, as if Azure had failed to understand an important truth. "You have your necklace, so you don't get it. If you didn't, you'd understand that we can do anything as founders. We have control over people's minds. Isn't that right, my lovely Ata?"

The wizard nodded at once. "That's correct, master."

Now his situation made sense. A wizard wouldn't knowingly serve vampires. He was being forced. And they hadn't turned him because they needed his magic. Azure had to find a way to break the mind control, though. She had to release Ata. That was going to be difficult, since he currently had her magically bound.

"Well, I've really enjoyed our first meeting, and can't wait for many, many more." Cordelia reached out again to pet Azure's head, and her hand hovered an inch away before she pulled it back. "I daresay it will be nice to have a woman around. Hamilton is lovely, but there are only so many things he can understand. It's been too long since I shared the company of another founder besides my love." She indicated the man, who stood and straightened his suit.

"Do you need my help rounding up the wizard and the Light Elf?" Hamilton asked.

Cordelia thought for a moment. "I don't need your help, but I do think I'd enjoy your company. So yes, please come along to fetch our next coven members. Our first new founders in over a century."

Azure screamed again, tears welling. How could she be so helpless? "Please don't. Leave Ever and Monet out of this. I'll become a vampire. I'll do whatever you say. Just leave them alone. Leave my people alone."

Cordelia clicked her tongue three times and shook her head. "What you don't understand is that you're going to do what we say no matter what. We don't settle or negotiate. We're vampires. We get what we want. We're going to have you, your friends, and your kingdom of witches and wizards." She smiled with a diabolical look in her eyes, her sharp fangs showing. "It's going to be simply lovely, my sweet. You just wait and see."

Hamilton offered his arm to Cordelia, who took it appreciatively as they turned to Ata. The wizard stepped out to the hallway at once. "Please keep her restrained, and continue to work on removing the necklace."

"Yes, master. It won't take long. I will try to have it done by the time you return," Ata said, his voice flat but still sounding like Chibale's.

"Very good." Cordelia turned back to Azure as she grabbed the doorknob. "Please get some rest, Queen Azure. When we return, your change will take place. I simply cannot wait." The vampire flashed Azure a wide smile, her large brown eyes twinkling. Then she shut the door, and a force she couldn't control made Azure lie flat again. She stared at the ceiling, frantic worry overtaking her chest and stress crowding her head. If she could have cried she might have, but all she could do was blink at the ceiling, breathe, and talk.

"It's going to be okay. It's going to be okay. It's going to be okay," she repeated to herself.

S tretching out, Monet plopped his feet on the coffee table. Laurel eyed his dirty shoes with disapproval before returning to scratching notes on a pad.

"You remind me a bit of Gillian, writing notes as we journey." Monet stirred the olive in his martini before taking a sip.

"You miss the old gnome, don't you?" Ever asked, sitting next to Monet with his own feet out and a drink in his hand as well.

"I wouldn't tell you if I did, but I *will* tell you that I'm curious what the short guy is up to. Hope he's not running the Potions Shop into the ground," Monet said.

"You know he isn't," Laurel said, more censure on her face. She took herself quite seriously, but Monet was working on breaking that nasty habit.

"You could try scrying him," Ever offered.

Monet gave him a look of disgust. "But then I'd have to get up and go all the way over there to the scrying bowl. I'd have to pour a potion into it, and use magic. That all sounds rather exhausting."

"And you can't be bothered to do anything, can you?" Laurel asked, absentmindedly petting Manx, who was currently a giant black dog. He had curled up at her feet. "I'm not sure it's wise for you two to get drunk while the queen is on Earth. She could need our help at any moment. Didn't you say you were supposed to go after her at some point if she didn't return?"

Monet eyed his watch and yawned. "Yes, but not yet. We have plenty of time to get drunk." He held out his martini glass to Ever, who clinked his against it appreciatively.

"One day I'm going to get you an iWatch or an iPhone so you can check up on Gillian and stay connected. I just have to figure out how to get reception on Oriceran. There's got to be a way." Ever muttered the last part to himself like he was thinking about a solution.

"Yeah, tell me more about this phone business… Is that connected to that Bookface thing?" Monet asked.

Ever laughed. "Facebook. And yes, social media is connected, and people use certain devices to access it."

Monet picked his olive out of his drink and threw it at the werecat, and she growled in disgust. "Ever was telling me that on Earth people post about their lives on this Facebook thing. They put up pictures of themselves and tell people what they're doing. What did you call the photos again?" he asked Ever.

"Selfies," the Light Elf supplied.

"Yes! They take selfies and put them up for everyone to see. 'I'm at the pub checking out a hot witch.'" He smiled broadly and then winked, as if posing for his own selfie. "People on Earth have nothing going on in their lives, it seems."

Manx awoke, sat up, and scooped the olive from the couch, eating it happily. Laurel shook her head at the pooka. "I don't get it. Why would anyone care?"

Ever took a sip of his martini. "Social media allows everyone to be obsessed with what everyone else is doing. There's a lot of posting, and maybe a little less living because of their need to document everything. It's become an addiction. Another reason I prefer Oriceran—things are simpler here."

Monet pulled his wand from his robes and waved it, and a potion bottle on the far side of the room lifted into the air and poured its contents into a scrying bowl. When the bottle was empty, the bowl flew across the room and landed on the coffee table beside Monet's feet.

"That looked so incredibly hard. Are you all right?" Laurel asked, mocking the wizard.

"I'm fucking exhausted, but I think I'll survive. The author of this story hasn't killed me off yet," Monet said, sitting up. Confusion covered Laurel's face, but Monet ignored it, stirring the potion with his wand.

"Oh, Gill-gill! Where are you?" Monet sang, looking into the scrying bowl.

The green potion swirled as shapes took form in it, then the liquid turned gray and Gillian's head swam into view. "Monet, is that you?"

"It is." He tapped the side of the scrying bowl with his wand and the image sharpened.

"Oh, now I can see you," the gnome said, looking as he

normally did with his brown bowler hat pressed onto his bald head.

"How's it going there, Shorty?" Monet asked.

Gillian ignored the joke. "We're out of creaseworms and rat spleen. I put in a new order, but we have some grumpy customers who don't want to wait a few days."

"Give them a dose of flubber scum. It will make them forget their troubles," Monet advised.

"How's Blisters? Is he of help to you?" Ever asked, leaning forward to peer into the bowl.

Gillian gave him a long cold look. "I think we all know the answer to that question. You thought I needed assistance running the shop so you assigned Blisters to help me? Really?"

Monet covered his laugh by taking a drink. "I thought of it as a teambuilding activity. He assists you, and Buzz Buzz assists him."

At the mention of her name the pixie flew into the frame, her fists shaking in the air and an angry look on her face. She let out what sounded like a series of complaints, but none of her words were understandable. As she whirled in a circle she pointed dramatically at her back, where her wings fluttered wildly.

"What's the fairy going on about?" Monet asked.

"Apparently Manx glued her wings together the morning you left. She couldn't fly for a whole day, which meant she had to walk around Virgo. She was nearly trampled several times. I figured out a potion to unstick her wings, but not until more damage was done," Gillian explained.

Laurel popped Manx on the nose. "You mean old

pooka. Why do you have to be so rotten to that pixie?"

"It's a fairy thing. You wouldn't understand," Manx said, stretching and shaking his black fur.

"More damage? What happened?" Ever asked.

"Well, Blisters felt bad for Buzz Buzz, so instead of finding a reasonable solution he decided to drink an entire bottle of shrinking potion," Gillian said, looking at something beside the bowl.

Monet laughed loudly, nearly doubling over.

"Oh, no, an entire bottle? Is he okay?" Laurel asked.

"I think so, but that's the thing. I don't know for sure, because I can't find him," Gillian said with a shrug. "Buzz Buzz was there when he drank the potion, and then he disappeared. I could give him the antidote, but for that I'd have to be able to see him." Gillian looked around, searching the shop for the microscopic unicorn.

Through his laughter Monet said, "He's a speck of dust, but don't worry. The potion will wear off in a couple of days and he'll slowly start to get bigger. By next week he'll be able to sit in the palm of your hand."

"That's awful. Will he be all right?" Laurel asked, shock on her face.

"He'll be fine. Just watch where you step, and don't give him the antidote. Unicorns are sensitive to potions, which is why it had such a dramatic effect on him. They amplify the potion's magic with their own," Monet explained.

Gillian scratched his head and nodded. "Okay. So yeah, Blisters hasn't really been a problem since I can't find him. The shop has mostly been quiet since you left. How is the trip?"

"It's great. I've been drunk since I woke up. Laurel has

taken on your role of offering me disapproving stares, and Azure went through a tear to Earth-Egypt because we're being hunted by vampires." Monet ran through all this pretty quickly and matter-of-factly.

"What did you say? *Hunted by vampires?* Is Azure okay?" Gillian's green eyes widened with sudden shock.

"I also said that I'm drunk, so I can't really remember what else I said," Monet said, emptying his glass.

"Azure's not with you?" Gillian asked.

"No, the ditz left us behind to find a cure or something for vampirism," Monet said in a monotone voice. "She apparently can see the tears between New Egypt and Egypt, and has a magic necklace from Mage Lenore. And she's getting all this attention from the coven here because the vampires want her. It's all quite boring. How's the slow-brew potion I was working on coming along? Is it bubbling yet?"

Gillian looked at Ever. "Is all this true? Tell me everything."

Monet waved his hand at the gnome and sat back on the couch.

Ever leaned forward. "Yes, it's true. There's an epidemic of vampirism here. The coven covered the whole thing up, afraid of scaring people away from New Egypt. There's at least one founder vampire that we know of, who is creating followers. The river has been telling this coven things about Azure and the vampires. Apparently, by going through the tear she'll find something that could aid in the battle against the vampires. Do you have any idea what that could be?"

Gillian's rubbed his face anxiously and nodded. "This

isn't good. The queen should have come back immediately upon learning of these vampires. If she's bitten, it will ruin the kingdom."

"Magic necklace, remember?" Monet said in a sing-song voice, pulling the knife Azure had given him out of his robe's inner pocket.

"Right...Mage Lenore. I remember now," Gillian said, sounding breathless. "And yes, I'm sure there's something in the Book of the Dead that explains how vampirism works and how it can be cured. However, the pages that document that were lost long ago. Vampires were suspected to be behind it. Obviously they didn't want that information found, so they stole the pages and now they are rumored to be lost forever."

"Well, Azure went through to Egypt. She might find something," Ever said hopefully.

"And even if the pages from the Book of the Dead were found, it's incredibly difficult to read." Gillian continued to speak as if he hadn't heard the Light Elf, his eyes distant.

"Could *you* interpret the pages?" Ever asked.

Gillian's eyes shot straight forward, shock covering his face. "Me? I'm not sure, although I guess I could try. I might be able to call in a favor from the Light Elf library."

"We'll let you know more when we hear from Azure. We're hoping she'll return soon, but she has to find another tear to get back here," Ever said.

"Yes, these tears between the worlds... I've heard of them, and they worry me. You *do* understand how they work?" Gillian asked.

"I don't think we understand much at this point," Ever

related, now watching Monet as he twiddled the knife in his hands.

"Tears are the vampires' method of travel between the sister kingdoms," Gillian began. "They can't take portals because they have no magic, but in the Egypts they can create tears. That's the only place they can create these passages between the worlds. You see, when the gods fought over the vampires, there was a certain balance struck. Ra, the sun god, said that vampires couldn't walk in the daylight. Osiris, the god of resurrection, brought the vampires back to life and gave them immortality. Geb, the god of Earth, decided they shouldn't be confined to that world, so he made it so they could pass through but only in the kingdoms where they originated, Egypt and New Egypt. Isis, the goddess of magic, took their magic from them. Horus, the god of war, made them hungry for blood. You see, the Egyptian gods control all aspects of the vampires, making the Egypts the best and worst place for them."

"That was what Chibale said. They are most powerful here, and also it's where their greatest weakness lies," Ever said, thinking.

"And if Azure can see tears, which continue to show up even after a vampire has left, then she's in essence following their path," Gillian said, his voice shaking.

"Which means she's bound to run into one," Ever said, his voice suddenly rising with fear.

Someone rapped at the door, making Laurel start slightly.

"Our pizza is here. We've got to ring off, old buddy. I'll follow back up with you later about the shop," Monet said, pushing the knife back into his pocket and picking up his wand.

"Wait! You have to let me know about Azure. The queen mother will be worried, and—"

"Easy solution—don't tell Gran about this. Catch ya later," Monet sang, tapping the side of the scrying bowl to make Gillian's image disappear.

Again the knock sounded at the door, this time a bit more forcefully.

Azure muttered under her breath, running through every spell she could remember to find one that would free her from Ata's restraints. She peered at the corner where her bag lay. She was fairly certain that if she could get her wand she could free herself, but that was ironically not how this all worked.

The lamp!

The idea occurred to her so suddenly it made her heart skip. The lamp was in her bag, along with her wand.

She pulled in a deep breath and quietly whispered, "Bob?"

For a moment nothing happened. Azure was just about to say the genie's name a bit louder when smoke poured from her bag and shot straight over to where she lay on the bed. Bob's coughing started to fill the air.

"Shush," she urged, trying to shake her head but unable to. "Please stop coughing."

"Is that a wish?" Bob asked, his voice hopeful.

"No, it's a request. If you keep that up, a bad wizard is going to take you away from me," she said in a terse whisper.

"Bad wizard, you say?" Bob stroked his chin.

The door handle clicked before turning.

"Hide," Azure urged as the door swung open.

The smoke and Bob shot under the bed, disappearing at once. Ata's face appeared in the opening of the doorway, his eyes narrowed with anger.

"What's going on in here?" he asked.

Azure pretended to cough. "The dry desert is getting to my lungs. I think I need a glass of water."

"You may have nothing until my masters return," Ata said, crossing his arms on his chest.

Azure staged a coughing fit, really exaggerating the scratchy, hacking sound. "Imagine how pissed they'll be when they find out I passed out due to dehydration. I haven't had any water all day, and in the desert that can be lethal, am I right?"

Ata considered Azure for a moment, then held his strange crook up and flicked it. A glass of water materialized on the bedside table.

"Perfect. Now can you allow me to use my limbs so I can get to it?" she asked.

A sadistic smile curled the edges of the wizard's mouth. "No need for that." He flicked his wand again and the glass floated through the air. Azure was pulled to a sitting position, and the glass tipped water into her mouth. Awkwardly her head went back, directed by the strange force that had laid her flat before.

Damn it! This fucking wizard wasn't going to allow her any freedom.

After a moment the water floated back to the bedside table.

"You know they are controlling you with their minds, right? You don't have to follow them. I could help you. I could return you to your coven. Chibale could help you. I know him," Azure said, and to her horror she heard Bob under the bed humming quietly. That fucking genie. Was he trying to get her killed? *Oh yeah, that's right,* she remembered. *Of course he was.*

"Chibale? He can't help me. He wouldn't. He's the reason I'm in this position, forced to serve these founder vampires," Ata said, his words on fire with vengeance.

"Chibale? The leader of the New Egyptian coven? Are you sure? He's trying to fight the vampires," Azure said, unsure what she was missing.

"Yes, I'm certain. However, he didn't realize what sort of danger I'd be put in when he forced me out into the desert. You see, I was the leader before him, but he put a spell on me that made me lose my mind. I ventured out into the desert, forgetting who I was and where my home could be found. I was lost.

Chibale hoped that he'd grow in power while I was away so that he could take the throne. However, while I was lost my masters found me and made me serve them. Chibale got what he wanted, but has no idea that I'm the one who has been forced to help the vampires. It's because of him that the vampires have taken over. It's because of him that I have to hold you prisoner. With me in their service my masters are very strong," Ata said, his voice haunted.

"These vampires are taking over *your* people." Azure's heart suddenly ached. How horrible this all was. The power-plays had been these wizards' very undoing. Azure observed that Ata's face was covered completely with tattoos, unlike Chibale's, which was only partially covered. This wizard was much stronger than the current coven leader.

"Yes, and my brother will be helpless to fight the vampires because they have me. I'm bound to them, and my power is unmatched," Ata imparted, his tone cursed.

"Brother?" Azure said. She'd observed how much the two looked like each other originally, but had dismissed it. "He's your twin, isn't he?"

"That is correct. We, like the Egyptian kingdoms, are connected, and he used that power to spell me with confusion. For weeks I roamed New Egypt, seeing it as the original Egypt looks. That was what kept me confused for so long," Ata confessed.

"That's horrible. Why would he do such a thing?" Azure asked.

"Because power is everything to our coven. Leaders die defending their claim to the throne. Chibale has always wanted to be king."

Azure shivered. "And this twin power... Why is it so prevalent here?" She thought of Nenet and Nefertiti and the two kingdoms.

"It's what the river deems. The river splits many things: the kingdom, our people, and vampires and bats. The magic of the river created the sister kingdoms. As long as the magic flows between them there will always be these splits," Ata explained.

Azure thought of her other half, Monet. She had to get out of there and help him. Her heart felt like it fell out of her chest when she thought of Ever and losing him to vampirism. She had to help them before it was too late. "If your brother knew what had happened to you, could he help?"

Ata shook his head. "I don't think anyone can help me now. As long as my masters are in power, I must do everything they say. There's no releasing me from my role as their servant. Their mental control is too strong."

Azure nodded solemnly. Ata was there in front of her. She could see the man, the wizard, under the shell he presented. Under the robot, forced to act, was the heart and soul of the once-leader of the New Egypt coven, but he had been buried by mind control and couldn't escape. Not yet, at least.

"Thanks for the water," Azure said, meaning it.

He nodded minutely, then pivoted and marched out of the room. When the door had closed the humming under the bed stopped and Bob rose, his eyes wide.

"That was a close one," he said in a loud whisper.

"Yes, you realize the severity of the situation. Is that why you were singing to yourself?" Azure asked, still unable to move.

"That's what I do when I get bored, which is basically all the time. It's quite tedious hanging around inside a lamp. However, *you* wouldn't know about that, would you, master? You've got this big world to stroll around in. Actually, I hear you have *two* worlds. Must be nice," Bob said bitterly.

"Would you stop the pity party for a moment? I need to get out of here, but I'm currently paralyzed. I need my bag and my wand, and I need to be released from this enchantment."

"That sounds like a couple of wishes," Bob said, gleefully. "I'll grant those right away and then I'll be gone for good."

"Wait, no," Azure whispered frantically. She wasn't sure why, but she couldn't release the genie yet. That was what using her remaining wishes would do. It would send Bob back to his lamp and then it would hide itself somewhere on Oriceran again. "On second thought, I only wish that you would release me from this restraining spell."

Bob's excited face fell with disappointment. "Oh, just the one wish...too bad. I'm starting to like you, and the longer I hang around you, the stronger the urge to kill you becomes. Call it a curse."

"Bob, will you shut up and grant my damn wish already?" Azure whispered.

"Fine, fine. You want to be free from a restraining curse. Most people want fame, money, good looks, and big muscles. My master only wishes to get herself out of trouble. So very boring." Bob rolled his turban-covered head on his shoulders, stretching his neck, then he flicked his head in her direction. Like coming out of a cast, Azure's muscles felt free. She flexed her fingers and her thumb brushed against her other digits.

"Perfect," she said, pushing off the bed and grabbing her bag. She pulled her wand out and stared around the room.

She had to figure out how to get out of there, but that wouldn't be easy. A powerful wizard guarded the other side of the door.

Bob, reading her expression of confusion, said, "What's the plan, master? You need to use another wish?"

If Monet had taught her how to use that disappearing and relocating spell she could get have gotten out of there, but there'd been no time for it.

"No, I don't need any more wishes. I've got a plan."

"Are you walking through that door? Because that's my vote. That wizard will probably strike you dead, and it will be too late for you to use your last wish. Maybe then I'll be free. I've never had a master die before using all their wishes," Bob said eagerly.

"No, it doesn't involve going through the door." Azure turned and held up her wand. "I'm going through the walls."

2 0

When Monet pulled open the door, a woman with a pleasing rack and a beautiful face was staring at him. The woman wore her black curls over her bare shoulders, and her fitted blue dress hugged her hips. She batted her eyelashes and smiled broadly, not showing her teeth.

"Hello, Beautiful. Yes, you've come to the right place," he said coolly, opening the door wide.

The woman's skin was pale—almost too pale. Monet picked up a strange scent from her, something that told him she was different. He covered his observation as a man, finely dressed, stepped from the hallway and stood next to the woman.

"Oh, I see it's not one of those deals. If you two don't have a pizza, I'm afraid I have lost my interest in you," Monet said, silently studying the man. He heard Ever rise from the couch behind him, and Manx' wings flapped as he shifted to raven form. Laurel moved as well.

"Isn't he lovely? I adore the green hair," the woman said,

extending her hand to Monet. "You may call me Cordelia. So nice to finally make your acquaintance, Monet."

Ever was now by the door and stared intently at the couple. Monet didn't take Cordelia's hand, but slid his own into the pocket of his robes to find the knife.

"This must be Ever. So handsome! I daresay you'll be even finer when we're done with you." The woman's eyes became hypnotic, drawing both men's attention to her. She was suddenly mesmerizing, as if she'd placed a spell on them. Monet found himself being sucked into her. Whatever she said next he would no doubt do. He'd do anything that she asked him to. Forever. For always. She owned him.

"You two will—"

The sound of flapping wings filled the air, and Manx darted over their heads and dove at the couple. They stepped back, shielding themselves as he launched at them, his clawed feet first. The man slammed his fist hard against the raven and Manx fell to the ground, where he lay limp.

Monet stepped backward during the commotion so that Ever was right beside him. They looked at each other, and in that moment they came to an understanding. They knew what had almost happened, and what could still happen if they weren't careful. Monet shoved the knife into Ever's hand and pulled out his wand. The Light Elf seemed to understand, and took a fighting stance.

The two vampires pushed their way into the suite. Laurel had a stick from the wood pile in her hand. She had pulled it from the fire, and it was burning at the end. With a strange new fierce look in her eyes the werecat ran for the vampires, brandishing the fire. She yelled like a warrior in battle.

Unflustered, Cordelia lifted her hand and Laurel rose off the ground several inches. She flailed, her legs kicking only air underneath her. Cordelia pushed her hand forward hard and Laurel shot back into a bookcase, where she slid to the ground, the fire extinguished by the force. Her head sank to the side; the impact had knocked her out instantly.

Cordelia unhurriedly looked back at Ever and Monet.

"Now, we could have done this the easy way, but it looks like we've decided to be uncooperative," she said playfully, like they were playing a game. "As I was saying—"

Monet threw his wand up and directed it at the vampires, yelling, "*Non-animi imperium.*"

A loud *crack* filled the room, followed by a huge cloud of smoke.

Cordelia opened her mouth and then slammed it shut, looking irritated. She gazed at the man. "Hamilton, he's stalled our mind control. What a crafty wizard!"

"It won't last long—those spells never do. Only another few seconds," Hamilton said. He stared at Ever, who had the knife out and pointed at him.

"We have your sweet Azure. She asked that we fetch you. You can come willingly or with force, but you *will* come." Cordelia wrapped her arms around her body as if giving herself a hug. "We're going to be such a happy family! You will all see."

The spell was wearing off—Monet could feel it. He searched for another way to fight these vampires. His potions were on the table in the corner, but there was nothing there that he thought would work. He backed up in unison with Ever as Cordelia and Hamilton advanced on them.

"Azure doesn't want to be a vampire, but when you two have been turned she'll beg to join you. That's how it works. We've seen it time and time again," Cordelia said, pausing and looking at the table of potions curiously.

She reached for a bottle of blue liquid. "Tick-tock. Your spell is almost over, and then it's our turn to play with your minds."

Monet narrowed his eyes at the potion, trying to remember which one it was, and in the cauldron on the table he saw something move. He twitched in sudden nervousness. There was something inside the empty cauldron, but what?

Hamilton looked at his watch. "Five, four, three, two, and—"

From the black cauldron something leapt, a howling sound ripping from its mouth. It was black and white, and its claws were extended. Then Monet saw it clearly: Finswick landed on Cordelia's back, his claws piercing her shoulders.

She screamed, mostly from shock, and dropped the potion to the ground, where it exploded. She scrambled to get the cat off her, but Finswick had already jumped away and vanished under the sofa. Ever had taken this opportunity to dart forward with the knife, and he thrust it straight into Hamilton's chest. The vampire stumbled back, his face shocked. His hands grabbed the hilt and frantic worry covered his face. He tugged once, twice...three times at the blade.

"Hamilton my love, is that..." Cordelia rushed to him

and grabbed the blade, pulling it from his chest. She held it up, her eyes fuming. "An orc's blade? No!"

Hamilton's hands covered his chest as he sucked in a breath. "It nearly killed me, but it missed my heart." He looked at Ever, wicked triumph on his face. "You've lost your chance. The next blow will be mine, and I won't miss." The vampire seemed to be fading, the knife wound having greatly injured him, but he lifted his hands to his side. *Crack.* Hamilton disappeared, replaced by a flying bat. Its wings beat the air before it darted out the open door.

Cordelia turned to Ever, venom in her smoldering brown eyes. "You nearly killed my lover, and now you will pay with your lives. I thought you would join us in eternal life, but I've changed my mind. Instead of becoming a member of our coven, you will simply be my dinner."

The vampire looked at Monet, and again he felt the strange trance settle over him. "Monet, you are under my influence and will do—"

Thundering footsteps filled the hallway, overwhelming Cordelia's voice.

Monet and Ever backed up farther, both intently focused on the doorway. What was approaching? It was loud. Menacing. Sounded destructive as it approached.

Cordelia impatiently looked at the hallway, her hands on her hips, and the head of a green dragon appeared in the doorframe. It narrowed its eyes on the vampire, flicking its forked tongue at her.

Cordelia started and backed up as well. The dragon brought its body around to join its head. Its shiny green scales caught the light; they were beautifully iridescent. Searching frantically for another way out—one that wasn't blocked by a dragon—she shot her hand at the bank of windows on the far wall, shattering them. Cool night air leaked into the suite, along with the sounds of the busy street below.

The dragon let out a horrible screech and its wings unfolded, nearly knocking into the walls close by. It rocked onto its hind legs, wings still outstretched, and when it came down the ground under it shook, making the building rock violently and sending objects flying off the shelves. Books fell onto Laurel's unconscious body and Monet and Ever stared at each other, unsure if they should fight the dragon or the vampire. Then, divining what was going to happen next, Monet grabbed Ever by the arm and yanked him hard to the side, darting behind the sofa to use it as a shield.

The dragon opened its mouth and let out another ear-splitting shriek, followed by a blast of white-hot fire. It filled the space where they'd just been.

At first Monet was certain Cordelia had been torched, but then over the rush of the fire he heard the squeak. Flying close to the ceiling was a tiny black bat. She beat her wings hard and dove, nearly flying into Monet's face. Her claws scratched his forehead and tugged through his hair before she escaped through the broken windows.

Monet and Ever felt the warm heat from the fireplace at their backs and the stinging fire blasted in front of them. The dragon closed its mouth, extinguishing the fire at once. Still, everything the fire had touched was ablaze.

Monet aimed his wand at the dragon, unsure if he should attack it. The creature darted its black eyes to him, a curious, almost taunting expression on its ancient face.

Then Oak appeared behind the dragon, wand in hand. He flicked it at the fires, making them all go out at once.

Everyone was silent for several seconds, the two men doing their best to breathe, having covered their faces against the smoke. Oak surveyed the space, his eyes studying every aspect.

"That's *your* dragon?" Ever said, both a question and a realization.

Oak reached down and scooped up something. "Of course she is. I thought she might be of use, since vampires hate fire. It reminds them of their eternal damnation."

The wizard strolled forward, the limp raven form of Manx in his hands. "The little guy is breathing, but will need mending. He took an awful blow, it appears."

Monet rushed forward, taking the pooka from him. "I have a potion that should help. I'll administer it right away. See to Laurel, please."

At that same moment the werecat stirred and pushed away from the bookcase. She stared in bewilderment at the chaos around her, and at the dragon who had curled up on the floor and was taking up a large section of the room. "What happened?" she asked, finding Ever by her side. Sparks of light had trailed behind him as he quickly moved to assist her.

"That's my question as well. Oak, how did you know to help us?" Ever asked, helping Laurel to her feet.

"I saw a bat fly from the main entrance. I was just outside, readying the carriage. I knew there was trouble brewing in here, especially after the vampire attack the other night, so I decided to bring Micky up here to investigate. She loves a field trip and hates vampires." Oak indicated the dragon, who looked beautifully peaceful, her head resting on her front legs, her horned tail gently flicking. Dragons were certainly majestic creatures, more intriguing than almost anything on Oriceran.

Monet filled a dropper with potion and squirted the contents into Manx' mouth after opening his beak with his fingertips. The raven stirred, but was still insensible.

"Will he be all right?" Ever asked, one arm around Laurel's shoulders.

"He needs rest, but yes, he will be fine," Monet said. He disappeared into a side room and returned with a towel, wrapping the bird in it and cradling him against his chest.

"He can't stay here. None of you can." Oak snapped at the dragon, who lazily lifted her head and stared at him with droopy eyes. "I'll take you to the carriage. You'll be safe there for the night. There're enchantments on it which none can break. No vampires will get to you while you're inside."

The dragon stood, seeming to understand, and slipped through the doorway into the hall. The group nodded, following Oak as he led the way. Monet grabbed a bottle of vodka from the case next to a side table, but he stopped in the entrance.

"Are you coming?" he said to the seemingly empty room.

Finswick peeked from under the couch. "I was going to catch up. I'm kind of enjoying my freedom."

"I was wondering when you were going to turn up. Just been lurking around, have you?" Monet asked playfully.

"I've been keeping an eye on things between my own

adventures," Finswick said, strolling out from under the couch. He looked up at Monet when he reached his feet.

"Thank you for attacking that hot-ass vampire. I nearly succumbed to her control," Monet said, readjusting Manx in his arms.

"You're welcome. I'll always have your back, or will jump onto the back of the offending vampire to help you out," Finswick said.

"You should come with us tonight. Azure will want to see that you're safe when she returns," Monet said, looking at the devastated suite. It was utter chaos. The bank of windows on the far side was completely gone, and glass covered the floor. The bookshelves were in complete disarray, and fire had singed a large portion of the room.

"*When* she returns. Are you certain of that? I heard what Cordelia said. She has her," Finswick said, real worry in his words.

"Yes, *when* she returns. They may have her, but she will find a way to escape. And if she isn't here by morning as we agreed, then I'll mow their kingdom down to find her."

21

Azure appraised the wall before her and put her ear to the surface, listening hard for any sounds on the other side. She was sure she'd heard something from the adjacent wall, which meant someone occupied the space.

She'd been given the idea for her plan by the barrier walls in the Sphinxes. What she was planning wasn't an easy spell, especially without muttering the incantation, but she couldn't risk Ata's hearing her. She felt a pang of guilt toward the wizard, who was being held hostage by Cordelia and Hamilton. She wanted to free him, release him from his enslavement, and she would—but not yet.

Thinking of enslavement reminded her of Bob. She'd considered asking him to release Ata and then it would be a win-win, but she was pretty certain that the genie would say it violated Section Thirty-three of Article Whatever. No, she'd have to find a different way to free Ata. Truthfully she had to fight the root cause of the problem first or

Cordelia and Hamilton would just find another witch or wizard to enslave. At least she knew Ata now, and more importantly she knew the history that had started this new epidemic.

Azure stepped back and secured her bag across her chest. Bob had retreated into his lamp, where hopefully he'd stay quiet. Aiming her wand at the wall, she mouthed an incantation.

The wall in front of her turned translucent and the other side came into view. To Azure's relief, the room was empty. She stepped through, feeling as though she were walking through a crowded wardrobe.

The wall solidified as soon as she was on the other side. This room was exactly like the one she'd been in. As she had suspected, this was a hotel.

With quick steps, she made her way to the far wall, but she could hear a murmur of voices on the other side so she checked the other wall. It was quiet, which was good news because this next room would have a different hallway than the one where Ata stood guard. He was Azure's major concern at this point, since he could paralyze her. The vampires couldn't touch her, but, as Lux had proven, they could knock her out.

Azure flicked her wand at the wall and again stepped through. She was halfway to the door when she heard a voice, "Queen Azure, what are you doing here?"

Azure whipped around to find Nenet sitting on the ground, rocking back and forth. Her feet were crossed, and her hands were resting on her knees as if she were in meditation. She was beside the bed, which was why Azure hadn't seen her when she entered the room.

"Nenet, you're here!" Azure checked her out. The new vampire looked as she had on the night she'd led them to the Sphinx.

"Yes, my founder lured me here the night we met. I've mostly been at this hotel ever since." A strange expression crossed her face. "Are you a vampire? Did I fail to recruit you to help Chibale?"

Azure shook her head. "No, I'm not a vampire."

"But I don't smell your blood or have the desire to feed on you, like I do with the living," Nenet said.

"It's my necklace. It protects me." Azure indicated the ruby hanging around her neck.

"Oh. Well, what are you doing here? Were you caught?" Nenet asked.

"Yes, but I'm trying to get away." She pointed to the door, which lead to a different hallway.

"I'm going with you, then," Nenet said, standing and grabbing a long shawl from the bed. She wrapped it around her head, her green eyes framed by the garment.

"You're going to leave? I didn't think that was possible."

"It isn't possible, or not for long, anyway. I can't leave Cordelia. I'm bound to her for all eternity. However, I *can* help you to escape," Nenet said.

"It sounds as though the person you were still lives inside you," Azure observed.

"I died and lost my magic. I have a thirst which kills. I think in time that the things I must do every day to survive as a predator will change me, make me cold and calloused, but for now I still remember what it felt like to live, breathe, and care for others. I still remember your kindness towards me. I still care for my people, and most of all for my sister. Those emotions have not yet faded," Nenet said, her words like the verses of a sad song.

"And you think those feelings and memories will fade over time?" Azure asked.

"Tonight I drank the blood of an old man. He was feeble and going to die soon, but my bite would have killed him in a few days even if I hadn't taken all his blood. A person cannot do these things on a daily basis and keep their humanity," Nenet stated, her voice haunted by what she'd done.

"And you might not always have the choice of who you feed on," Azure said, and regretted it almost at once.

The horror that sprang to Nenet's eyes was chilling. "Yes. I chose the old man carefully, and was given that luxury because my thirst wasn't overwhelming. I'm a monster, though, and will not always be able to control my cravings. In the wrong company, I might hurt those who are truly innocent, the young. I might hurt those who are truly good and powerful, taking them from this world forever."

Azure grasped Nenet's shoulders. "I'm working to help you. I can make no promises, but I will do everything I can to free you from this curse. Chibale and I are working together."

"If you're here, then you've met Ata and know that Chibale is a traitor. He should be punished for what he did. We all followed him blindly when King Ata disappeared. We didn't know," Nenet said, her tone hot with anger.

"Chibale made a mistake. Yes, he was selfish and lusted for power, but you of anyone should know that sometimes we can't control our desires. He had no idea his spell would put Ata in such danger—I'm sure of that. Whether he is punished is not my decision, but this should be a time of great compassion for those who make mistakes. If we can't forgive them, then we will battle each other and the vampires will no doubt win," Azure said, resolution ringing in her speech, the words rushing out of her quickly and unrehearsed.

Nenet studied Azure for a moment, taking in her words, and finally she nodded. "I believe you might be right. My thirst makes it increasingly difficult for me to think clearly. I'm glad you spoke those words, which I needed to hear. Now I have words for you, Queen Azure." Nenet pulled a flail from the pocket of her gown. "This is twin to my sister's crook. Twins are issued these instead of wands in New Egypt because of the power we share. It's believed that the great pharaohs enhanced our powers by making us separate. I want you to return this to my sister Nefertiti. You *have* met her, have you not?"

"Yes," Azure said solemnly. "She misses you very much." Azure didn't think it a good idea to also mention how angry Nenet's twin was with her for being bitten.

"Since I no longer have my magic, Nefertiti should have my flail. Her crook will be stronger with this nearby."

"But she's not as strong as she was before, is she?" Azure asked.

"No. When I lost my magic, I decreased her power. I was a tributary to the river, and when I dried up the flow of magic diminished," Nenet explained.

"I'll return this to Nefertiti, do not worry." Azure accepted the flail and placed it in her bag.

"There's something else." Nenet reached out to touch

Azure, but the motion halted a few inches away. "As I've communicated to you, this life is not for me. It is torture. And although I might come to appreciate it in time, as Cordelia tells me I will, I don't want to become a monster."

Azure stepped back, sensing what the vampire was going to say next.

Nenet closed the space quickly, her eyes desperate. "Queen Azure, I believe you'll fight to find a solution, but if you don't then I have a request. If there is no way to save us, if vampires are truly doomed, then I need you to do something."

Azure's eyes widened in both shock and heartbreak. She found herself shaking her head before the request was even made.

"Yes, Queen Azure," Nenet said, nodding adamantly. "If you cannot save us, then I need you to kill me. You have to erase me from this world before I cause too much harm. Please, you must promise me that."

Azure almost choked on a sob, but swallowed it. How could she do this? Promise to kill Nenet when the time came? But how could she *not* grant this wish for peace to this woman? She was a witch, after all, and it could have been Azure who had been changed forever and made to thirst. Finally she nodded, unable to say anything.

"Thank you. Now we should get you out of here, if that's what you wish to do," Nenet strode for the door, listening.

The vampire turned, her face not at all hopeful. The white streak across her green eyes, her soul mark, chilled suddenly. "Queen, there are followers in the hallway. I hear the voices of Lux and Devo. They are the founders' most trusted minions. I think you should stay here until the vampires sleep at dawn. That would be the best time to escape."

Azure shook her head at once. "No, I have to go now. Cordelia and Hamilton have gone after my own, Monet and Ever. I have to help them, or at least join the fight." Azure was sure that Ever and Monet would put up a fight. She worried for them, but they were strong, and Monet had the orc's knife.

"Okay, I get it. I'd risk my life too, if it were Nefertiti," Nenet said.

"Lux does know who I am, though. He was the one who brought me here in the first place," Azure explained.

Nenet pulled the shawl from her head. "Then he'd recognize you. Place this over your blue hair and keep your head down. Stay at my side. There are others here, but they'll think you're one of them unless you draw attention to yourself."

Azure fixed the shawl over her head, tucking her hair under it. She gave a reassuring nod to Nenet just before she pulled open the door.

Broken furniture lined the hallway. The once-pristine walls of the hotel were scarred with marks of abuse, including long scratches.

Azure stepped into the hallway and on the other side met a vampire. He was tall, with narrow shoulders and a full head of brown hair. The man wore several loops in his eyebrows, nose, and lip. His beady eyes narrowed at the two girls and he threw a knife in their direction.

Azure's heart leapt and she ducked as the knife soared overhead.

"Devo! Are you mad, you fool?" Nenet yelled down the hallway to the man.

He laughed loudly. "Of course I am, but are you *dumb*? It's just a fun game."

"Throwing knives isn't a game," Nenet said, gesturing for Azure to get behind her.

"They can't really hurt you. That's why it's fun. You're a vampire—or don't you remember, newbie?" He pulled another knife from his belt and threw it.

Nenet reached out and grabbed it with incredible precision when it was just in front of her chest, and in one swift movement she flicked the knife in the opposite direction. It spiraled through the air and thunked straight into Devo's arm.

"Ouch! Damn it, you got me," he said, mostly laughing. He winced a bit in pain as he pulled the blade free. "See, it's a lot of fun!"

"You're an idiot, and you and Lux have destroyed the hotel. You'd do better to take care of it. This is our home," Nenet said, backing up. Azure tried to hide behind her inconspicuously.

"It's our home for *now*," Devo said. "We were given this floor to do what we liked, and I like to throw knives."

He unleashed another blade and it soared down the long hallway. Nenet reached for it but missed this time. The blade tore past her and through Azure's hair, nearly grazing the skin of her face.

She stumbled back, unnerved by the realization that she had nearly been stabbed.

"Who is that behind you?" Devo asked.

"It's no one," Nenet said too fast.

"No one? That's curious," the man said jovially.

"Devo!" Lux' voice rang from behind him.

"What?" he called.

"We've got to get ready to go to Lancothy. You said there were bats in the caves there?" Lux asked.

"Yep." Devo held up another knife, weaving it forward and backward through the air as if about to unleash it.

Lux appeared next to Devo, a frustrated expression on his face. He looked at him, and then followed his line of vision. At first Lux turned, not giving Nenet or the figure behind her much attention, but then he took a second look.

"Who is that with you, Nenet?" Lux asked.

"It's Maat," Nenet said, supplying a random name.

"Maat? We don't have a 'Maat.'" Lux strode forward, his expression curious.

Azure backed up quickly, nearly tripping on her own feet. She was almost to the bend in the hallway when a figure sprang between the two men.

"She's escaped! Queen Azure is loose," Ata yelled. He came to a sudden halt when he spied Azure at the other end of the hallway, a new fury on his face.

He lifted his crook and began muttering under his breath.

Nenet turned back to Azure. "Go! I'll hold him off!"

Azure took several steps backwards, recognizing the curse she heard him muttering. He was going to freeze her again, and this time she'd be unable to speak or open her eyes. He was going to imprison her for good.

"But—"

"*GO!* You have to get out of here," Nenet yelled, cutting her off.

Azure nodded and bolted in the opposite direction as she saw the young vampire launch herself at the wizard.

There was a great commotion. Shouting. Destruction. Banging. Nenet screamed in pain.

"Run, Queen Azure! *Run!*" Nenet yelled, and then everything went completely quiet.

Azure ran down the stairs, taking them two at a time. She burst into a great lobby, where several vampires stopped and regarded her with mild interest. Some were feeding on victims. Others lounged under windows through which the moon shone, and it bathed them in its light. Azure didn't stop running, leaping over bodies as she made her way to the exit.

From the other end of the room, a great shuffling echoed.

Azure turned back at the exit, knowing that she'd never make it through the city if she didn't do one last thing.

Ata was the first to disembark from the staircase, but she couldn't harm him. That would be like hurting an innocent person or a prisoner. Before he could raise his crook, Azure held her wand up and yelled, "*Somnum.*"

Ata, the target of her spell, swayed, stumbling forward and then backward. He teetered, trying to lift his crook and point it at her. He mumbled, but the right syllables didn't pass his lips. Then he fell forward, crashing hard onto his chest. The vampires around him fell over one by one, all of them hit by the sleep spell Azure had cast. She'd used all her reserves to ensure it worked and it had, so well that it had connected with Ata and everyone in his vicinity.

Feeling that she might fall asleep as well, Azure forced herself to turn for the exit. She burst into the open air of the New Egyptian night, where stars twinkled in the black sky and a foreboding silence met her ears.

22

A zure didn't stop running until she arrived at the hallway where her suite was located in her hotel, and then she nearly fell to her knees. The destruction outside the suite told her what she didn't want to know—she was too late. Cordelia and Hamilton had already been there.

There was a spot of blood just on the other side of the threshold. Black blood. Hadn't she heard that pookas bled black? Her heart sank.

In the doorway she saw more that brought questions to her mind. The scene seemed to tell an incomplete story, one her imagination tried to fill in. A destroyed bookshelf with contents scattered everywhere. Someone had been thrown into the shelf, maybe?

The bank of windows had been blown out and broken glass was everywhere. Had Monet used magic to destroy the windows? Why?

Fire damage scarred one wall. It had destroyed much of

the furniture, some of Monet's potion supply, and the paintings that had decorated the space. Someone had extinguished it before it had taken out Monet's vodka supply. Azure turned slowly, scanning the destruction as she wondered where her friends were. Did Cordelia and Hamilton have them? Was she too late? Would she become a vampire if that fate had already been forced on Monet and Ever? She almost thought she would, but there was her kingdom to consider.

Her eyes fastened on the ground, and then Azure bent down and retrieved the orc's knife. Its blade was covered in blood. Azure lifted it, eyeing it for any hints of what had happened in the battle tonight. She grabbed the hem of her gown and wiped the blade clean, and then her eyes flitted to the case of vodka. There was one missing—that she knew—so her friends were out there. They had to be. She pulled the knife close to her chest before launching through the suite and hallway and outside.

Azure was ready to run all the way back to the hotel she'd just escaped from, if necessary. She'd tear through it until she found her friends. Until she'd saved them. But given the missing bottle of vodka, she decided to stop at the stables just in case.

She sprinted, feeling the icy desert air on her exposed arms and chest. The knife was firmly clutched in her hands. She was aware that the white gown was covered in the blood from the knife, but she didn't care. Then the red and gold carriage came into view—it was still here! Even if nothing else had gone well, *it* was still here. Azure hadn't lost everything.

As she got nearer, she made out the figure in black

standing next to the carriage. Was that Oak? She didn't see the black hat on his head. All she saw was his black hair. But still, Oak was there. The dragons... Would they be in the stalls for the night? Questions continued to trail through Azure's mind as she neared the carriage.

In the glow of the moonlight, she saw the figure look up. He'd heard her footsteps on the bricks. It was like a dream. Better, actually. After everything she'd seen, the destruction she'd witnessed, this was the best thing she could have hoped for.

Relief broke across her face. The figure straightened, taking her in.

Azure halted, staring at Ever as if she were seeing him for the first time after a long journey. Had it only been this morning that she'd traveled to Earth and been abducted? She dropped the knife, unable to hold onto it any longer. Exhaustion would overwhelm her soon. The clattering of the metal on the pavement served to awaken the night and make the sun rise.

Ever stepped forward, running his eyes over the white gown stained with the blood of a vampire.

"Are you..." he tried to ask, but continued to study her.

She nodded. "Are you?"

He nodded and took an almost tentative step in her direction as if he were afraid she might vanish if he approached too quickly.

"Manx? I saw the blood. Is he..."

"He'll be fine," Ever said with a relieved smile on his face. "Everyone is fine, Azure. You're back, so we'll be okay."

And just like that he closed the space—like the curse

had been broken and he could grab her now. She allowed herself to be pulled in, allowed his arms to engulf her. Her heart suddenly beat faster and harder. She felt like she could finally rest after a long and horrible nightmare, Azure crashed into Ever, letting him absorb her body weight, and the two stayed like that for a long time, relieved they were all okay. They had survived, even as the night inched past with its curses lurking in every shadow, waiting to attack again.

EPILOGUE

When Cordelia and Hamilton strode into the lobby of the hotel, the sight that met their eyes was unacceptable at best. It spoke of further defeat. Not only had they failed to abduct Monet and Ever to add them to their coven as founders, they'd also lost the queen.

Cordelia marched over to the figure lying face-down by the stairs and toed Ata's unconscious body. He was breathing—she could hear that with her enhanced senses—but if he was here then Azure had escaped.

Lux and Devo had started to wake and now pushed themselves sluggishly to their feet. Many in the lobby were stirring, but Ata had been hit by the major blast and would not be able to use magic for a while. He stirred, but only slightly.

The damn witch had done this. She'd escaped, and her friends had eluded the ancient vampires. This was not how things were supposed to go.

Cordelia spun to face Hamilton. "We have failed." She mouthed the last as if it were a dirty word.

He ran a finger over a table and looked at the tip like he was inspecting it for dust. "On the bright side, this place has been compromised, so we can upgrade to a better one."

She pursed her lips. "Yes, I suppose you're right. We only have a bit more of the night, so we had better get a move on."

She clapped her hands, and like statues coming to life the half-dozen vampires in the room came to attention. They straightened, their eyes sharp and resting on Cordelia.

"Hamilton and I are going to find a new location. You all will stay here and prepare. When you are summoned, come to us," she said and turned to Lux, who was brushing his shirt off.

"You and Devo will follow us. Tomorrow night I want you in Lancothy. We need more bats," Cordelia ordered.

"You're not giving up on the queen, then?" Lux asked.

"Of course not. I'm even more determined now that she'll be ours." Cordelia moved toward the exit, taking Hamilton's arm as she passed him. She paused a few feet from the doors, but didn't turn. "Oh, and Ata?"

The wizard was just getting to his feet, the deep slumber having made him quite groggy. "Yes, master, I will stay here and watch over the coven. I will follow them to the new location when they are summoned. I am forever your faithful servant," Ata said, his voice robotic.

Cordelia offered a satisfied smile to Hamilton. "Isn't it wonderful, darling? Even when it all falls apart, we can so easily put it back together."

"Indeed, my love," Hamilton said as the two strode from the hotel.

FINIS

I did a very naughty thing. I abandoned my characters for a whole month, maybe more...I can't remember. If they were puppies, then I put them in a kennel and walked away, leaving them to hound at the gates as I slid into my RV and headed to the hills on vacation. Okay, you're wondering what I'm talking about? I'm wondering what I'm talking about. I didn't actually go on vacation, don't be crazy. I don't get one of those. The holidays came. Other projects too. My backlist told me it needed some air to breathe. What I'm saying is that I took a break from this series and it made me ever so lonesome for my Oriceran family. It wasn't easy to board these characters, but that's what my life called for.

The good news, for this horrible analogy that I've beaten over the head with a stick, is that I'm back. I missed Azure and the gang so much and when I let them back into my head they had so much to tell me. There's a flow to characters that a writer only finds when they've written multiple books with them. I'm starting to call it "hitting my stride". I've never written more than five books in a series, well, unless you count my Ren series (wow, shameless plug, much). I was surprised at how effortless the character voices came to me. It was like I was recording scenes rather than creating them.

I remember coming to Martha and Michael with this idea for vampires in New Egypt. The two were instantly supportive, as they always are. Michael was throwing out ideas so fast that I was completely encouraged. You see, I've always wanted to set a book, or a few, in Egypt. However, there's a lot of history and mythology to keep up with. Oriceran gave me the perfect place. I could pull from the Egyptian pharaohs and gods, and then tweak things to my liking. And better yet, I could create a parallel universe between the two. I'm getting giddy just thinking back on the creation of this all.

My daughter was a huge help with this series. I said "Egypt" to this kid and she was spitting out ideas so fast that I had to dry my soapy hands from washing dishes and start jotting down ideas. I wished I could tell you all the great ideas my six-year old gave me, but that's called spoilers. Those secrets will be revealed in other books. I will tell you that she gave me the idea for the genie. I was like, "You're a genius!" No, I didn't say "Gen-us". Then we had to name the genie. She had ideas, but this time I left it to the readers. I polled the fans on Facebook, join the Oriceran group if you haven't, and they had loads of great suggestions. Anyway, their suggestions will stretch across this arc, but let's give out some credit. First of all we had not one, but three entries that won the name of the genie.

Thank you to Sarah Weir, Cameron Scott Wright, Roy Sinclair for helping me name Bob, the evil genie who wants to murder Azure. I kind of like him, don't you? And then there were soooo many great names that I had to include them throughout the book as suggestions. Manx and Laurel just won't give it up that Bob should have a better name. So throughout the series they'll try and rename him. Ever and Monet will probably join in on the game. In book one though, we have suggestions for other names for the genie given by: Micky Cocker, Anne Loshuk, Ron Gailey, Amba Jane, Margaret Cambridge and Christa Stojanova.

Oh, and before I take up all the pages with my ramblings, a special thanks to James Caplan. He's become my champion, helping me a ton with ideas and encouragement. His ideas are constantly sneaking their way into my books. I'm starting to lose track. I count myself lucky that I have such awesome readers to help me on my author journey. Thank you to you all.

Sarah

Check out Sarah Noffke's Fantasy Series:

Vagabond Circus

A circus that is spellbinding, mesmerizing and deadly.

When a stranger joins the cast of Vagabond Circus--a circus that is run by Dream Travelers and features real magic--mysterious events start happening. The once orderly grounds of the circus become riddled with hidden threats. And the ringmaster realizes not only are his circus and its magic at risk, but also his very life.

Vagabond Circus caters to the skeptics. Without skeptics, it would close its doors. This is because Vagabond Circus runs for two reasons and only two reasons: first and foremost to provide the lost and lonely Dream Travelers a place to be illustrious. And secondly, to show the nonbelievers that there's still magic in the world. If they believe, then they care, and if they care, then they don't destroy. They stop the small abuse that day-by-day breaks down humanity's spirit. If Vagabond Circus makes one skeptic believe in magic, then they halt the cycle, just a little bit. They allow a little more love into this world. That's Dr. Dave Raydon's mission. And that's why this ringmaster recruits. That's why he directs. That's why he puts on a show that makes people question their beliefs. *He wants the world to believe in magic once again.*

AUTHOR NOTES - MARTHA CARR

WRITTEN DECEMBER 4, 2017

The Oriceran Universe is now almost five months old and it feels like I've always known Sarah Noffke and the other authors. The girl has busted a move to get out so many new stories. It has been fun to see how much all of us have grown and in such a short amount of time. Welcome to Michael Anderle's boot camp to become a successful author! There should be a shoulder patch of some kind. Maybe something Elven...

Now, we're at a place in the Universe where more infrastructure is needed – or maybe I have finally caught on a little better about how to market more consistently and do a better job of connecting with fans. Either way I have an action plan that feels pretty good.

I'm at the point where I need help to get all those new tasks done. And, since numbers are not my thing it's twice as important. Every time I hear Magic Mike or Craig talking about costs per click it translates to Klingon in my head.

Good news! I raised my own marketing genius! The offspring does this for a living for others and now that I know what to ask for – and since he came to the 20Books Convention in Vegas and saw on a deeper level what I do – he's cleaning up a lot of my act and helping out the Universe. That'll make the whole experience better for everyone with more to do, more to read and even easier to get to know all of us.

It's turning out to be a lot of fun to work with the offspring – Louie... The information is like kibble for him and he can take it all in, draw conclusions and spit out an action plan. Meanwhile, I'm still back there wondering what just happened.

It's a cool thing about this boot camp... all of us started the Universe with the idea that sure this'll work but we had no guarantees. And now, not only did you guys – THE FANS – show up, you've shown up in droves and all of us authors, like Sara Noffke and myself, have stretched and grown and learned so much about ourselves that we never expected and are really grateful we were here to do. More adventures to follow.

First, thank you so much for reading not only our tales, but all the way through the author notes to now, my publisher notes as well!

For shameless plugs, I'm going to provide Sarah and Martha's personal author pages. You can find them here:

Sarah Noffke: https://www.amazon.com/Sarah-Noffke/e/B00QQC5PFQ

Martha Carr: https://www.amazon.com/Martha-Carr/e/B001JP4SW6

If you are EVER in need of a story, then I highly recommend both of my collaborator's works. They can take you from Fantasy, to Urban Fantasy, to Thriller and beyond.

Without ever leaving the comfort of your favorite reading chair.

These two ladies are amazing in their writing, and wonderful in their lives. They care and support those around them equally.

While LMBPN Publishing (my company) does *NOT*

publish all of their books – they have their own publishing companies and other groups they publish with – I would love to encourage you to try out their personal works that have nothing to do with Oriceran.

(And then come back to Oriceran, just a suggestion...)

We are into the Christmas season, and I would be remiss to fail to mention that I appreciate all of the wonderful support you provide us here in the Oriceran Universe. To those mentioned in Sarah's Author Notes, and those names Martha has mentioned and the many, many others we interact with through each week, you are a blessing.

So, thank you from us, to you.

Now, I'm going to see if I really, really have to tweak that last chapter in my next book, or maybe I can get a story and do a little reading.

Because, as an author myself, I need to spend time in other people's books to help fill up my creative well.

Ad Aeternitatem,

Michael Anderle

- Rule of Magic (4) - Dealing in Magic (5) - Theft of Magic (6) -
Enemies of Magic (7) - Guardians of Magic (8)

The Soul Stone Mage Series

* Sarah Noffke and Martha Carr *

House of Enchanted (1) - The Dark Forest (2) - Mountain of
Truth (3) - Land of Terran (4) - New Egypt (5) - Lancothy (6) -
Virgo (7)

The Kacy Chronicles

* A.L. Knorr and Martha Carr *

Descendant (1) - Ascendant (2) - Combatant (3) - Transcendent
(4)

The Midwest Magic Chronicles

* Flint Maxwell and Martha Carr*

The Midwest Witch (1) - The Midwest Wanderer (2) - The
Midwest Whisperer (3) - The Midwest War (4)

The Fairhaven Chronicles

* with S.M. Boyce *

Glow (1) - Shimmer (2) - Ember (3) - Nightfall (4)

ABOUT SARAH NOFFKE

Sarah Noffke, an Amazon Best Seller, writes YA and NA sci-fi fantasy, paranormal and urban fantasy. She is the author of the Lucidites, Reverians, Ren, Vagabond Circus, Olento Research and Soul Stone Mage series. Noffke holds a Masters of Management and teaches college business courses. Most of her students have no idea that she toils away her hours crafting fictional characters. Noffke's books are top rated and best-sellers on Kindle. Currently, she has eighteen novels published. Her books are available in paperback, audio and in Spanish, Portuguese and Italian. http://www.sarahnoffke.com

THE LUCIDITES SERIES:
Awoken, #1:

Around the world humans are hallucinating after sleepless nights.

In a sterile, underground institute the forecasters keep reporting the same events.

And in the backwoods of Texas, a sixteen-year-old girl is about to be caught up in a fierce, ethereal battle.

Meet Roya Stark. She drowns every night in her dreams, spends her hours reading classic literature to avoid her family's ridicule, and is prone to premonitions—which are becoming more frequent. And now her dreams are filled with strangers offering to reveal what she has always wanted to know: Who is she? That's the question that haunts her, and she's about to find out. But will Roya live to regret learning the truth?

Stunned, #2

Revived, #3

THE REVERIANS SERIES:

Defects, #1:

In the happy, clean community of Austin Valley, everything appears to be perfect. Seventeen-year-old Em Fuller, however, fears something is askew. Em is one of the new generation of Dream Travelers. For some reason, the gods have not seen fit to gift all of them with their expected special abilities. Em is a Defect—one of the unfortunate Dream Travelers not gifted with a psychic power.

Desperate to do whatever it takes to earn her gift, she endures painful daily injections along with commands from her overbearing, loveless father. One of the few bright spots in her life is the return of a friend she had thought dead—but with his return comes the knowledge of a shocking, unforgivable truth. The society Em thought was protecting her has actually been betraying her, but she has no idea how to break away from its authority without hurting everyone she loves.

Rebels, #2

Warriors, #3

VAGABOND CIRCUS SERIES

Suspended, #1:

When a stranger joins the cast of Vagabond Circus—a circus that is run by Dream Travelers and features real magic—mysterious events start happening. The once orderly grounds of the circus become riddled with hidden threats. And the ringmaster realizes not only are his circus and its magic at risk, but also his very life.

Vagabond Circus caters to the skeptics. Without skeptics, it would close its doors. This is because Vagabond Circus runs for two reasons and only two reasons: first and foremost to provide the lost and lonely Dream Travelers a place to be illustrious. And secondly, to show the nonbelievers that there's still magic in the world. If they believe, then they care, and if they care, then they don't destroy. They stop the small abuse that day-by-day breaks down humanity's spirit. If Vagabond Circus makes one skeptic believe in magic, then they halt the cycle, just a little bit. They allow a little more love into this world.

That's Dr. Dave Raydon's mission. And that's why this ringmaster recruits. That's why he directs. That's why he puts on a show that makes people question their beliefs. He wants the world to believe in magic once again.

Paralyzed, #2
Released, #3

REN SERIES:

Ren: The Man Behind the Monster, #1:

Born with the power to control minds, hypnotize others, and read thoughts, Ren Lewis, is certain of one thing: God made a mistake. No one should be born with so much power. A monster awoke in him the same year he received his gifts. At ten years old. A prepubescent boy with the ability to control others might merely abuse his powers, but Ren allowed it to corrupt him. And since he can have and do anything he wants, Ren should be happy. However, his journey teaches him that harboring so much power doesn't bring happiness, it steals it. Once this realization sets in, Ren makes up his mind to do the one thing that can bring his tortured soul some peace. He must kill the monster.

Note This book is NA and has strong language, violence and sexual references.

Ren: God's Little Monster, #2
Ren: The Monster Inside the Monster, #3
Ren: The Monster's Adventure, #3.5
Ren: The Monster's Death

OLENTO RESEARCH SERIES:
Alpha Wolf, #1:

Twelve men went missing.

Six months later they awake from drug-induced stupors to find themselves locked in a lab.

And on the night of a new moon, eleven of those men, possessed by new—and inhuman—powers, break out of their prison and race through the streets of Los Angeles until they disappear one by one into the night.

Olento Research wants its experiments back. Its CEO, Mika Lenna, will tear every city apart until he has his werewolves imprisoned once again. He didn't undertake a huge risk just to lose his would-be assassins.

However, the Lucidite Institute's main mission is to save the world from injustices. Now, it's Adelaide's job to find these mutated men and protect them and society, and fast. Already around the nation, wolflike men are being spotted. Attacks on innocent women are happening. And then, Adelaide realizes what her next step must be: She has to find the alpha wolf first. Only once she's located him can she stop whoever is behind this experiment to create wild beasts out of human beings.

Lone Wolf, #2
Rabid Wolf, #3
Bad Wolf, #4

BOOKS BY MICHAEL ANDERLE

For a complete list of books by Michael Anderle, please visit

www.lmbpn.com/ma-books/

All LMBPN Audiobooks are Available at Audible.com and
iTunes. For a complete list of audiobooks visit:

www.lmbpn.com/audible

CONNECT WITH THE AUTHORS

Want more?
 Join the email list here:
 http://oriceran.com/email/
 Find the Oriceran Universe on Facebook:
 https://www.facebook.com/OriceranUniverse/
 Find the Oriceran Universe on Pinterest:
 https://www.pinterest.com/lmbpn/pins/

The email list will be a way to share upcoming news and let you know about giveaways and other fun stuff. The Facebook group is a way for us to connect faster – in other words, a chat, plus a way to share new spy tools, ways to keep your information safe, and other cool information and stories. Plus, from time to time I'll share other great indie authors' upcoming worlds of magic and adventure. Signing up for the email list is an easy way to ensure you receive all of the big news and make sure you don't miss any major releases or updates.

Enjoy the new adventure!

Sarah Noffke and Martha Carr 2017

Sarah Noffke Social

Website: http://www.sarahnoffke.com

Facebook: https://www.facebook.com/officialsarahnoffke

Amazon: http://amzn.to/1JGQjRn

Martha Carr Social

Website: http://oriceran.com/

Facebook:
https://www.facebook.com/ChroniclesofLeira/

www.ingramcontent.com/pod-product-compliance
Lightning Source LLC
Chambersburg PA
CBHW050247110726

47898CB00007B/2315